NEW YORK REVIEW BOOKS
CLASSICS

THE QUEUE

VLADIMIR SOROKIN was born in a small town outside of
Moscow in 1955. He trained as an engineer at the Moscow Institute of Oil and Gas, but turned to art and writing, becoming a
major presence in the Moscow underground of the 1980s. His
work was banned in the Soviet Union, and his first novel, *The
Queue*, was published by the famed émigré dissident Andrei
Sinyavsky in France in 1983. In 1992, Sorokin's *Collected Stories*
was nominated for the Russian Booker Prize; in 1999, the publi-
cation of the controversial novel *Blue Lard*, which included a sex
scene between clones of Stalin and Khrushchev, led to public
demonstrations against the book and to demands that Sorokin be
prosecuted as a pornographer; in 2001, he received the Andrei
Belyi Award for outstanding contributions to Russian literature.
Sorokin is also the author of the screenplays for the movies
Moscow, *The Kopeck*, and *4*, and of the libretto for Leonid
Desyatnikov's *The Children of Rosenthal*, the first new opera to
be commissioned by the Bolshoi Theater since the 1970s. He has
written eleven novels, as well as numerous plays and short stories, and his work has been translated throughout the world. He
lives in Moscow.

SALLY LAIRD is a translator from Danish and Russian and a
former editor of the magazine *Index on Censorship*. She is the
author of *Voices of Russian Literature* (1999), and her translations
from Russian include works by Ludmilla Petrushevskaya and
Igor Pomerantsev. She lives in Denmark.

THE QUEUE

VLADIMIR SOROKIN

Translated from the Russian and with a preface by
SALLY LAIRD

NEW YORK REVIEW BOOKS

New York

THIS IS A NEW YORK REVIEW BOOK
PUBLISHED BY THE NEW YORK REVIEW OF BOOKS
435 Hudson Street, New York, NY 10014
www.nyrb.com

Published in the Russian language as *Ochered'*
First published in 1985 by Syntaxis, Paris
First published in English by Readers International Inc., New York,

Library of Congress Cataloging-in-Publication Data
Sorokin, Vladimir, 1955–
  [Ochered'. English]
  The queue / by Vladimir Sorokin ; translated by Sally Laird.
      p. cm. — (New York Review Books classics)
  Originally published: New York : Readers International Inc., 1988.
  ISBN 978-1-59017-274-2 (alk. paper)
  I. Laird, Sally. II. Title.
PG3488.O66O2813 2008
891.73'44—dc22

                              2007052586

ISBN 978-1-59017-274-2

Printed in the United States of America on acid-free paper.
10 9 8 7 6 5

CONTENTS

PREFACE · vii
by Sally Laird

THE QUEUE · 1

AFTERWORD: FAREWELL TO THE QUEUE · 253
by Vladimir Sorokin

PREFACE

Twenty years have passed since the first edition of this translation was published,* and much has happened in the interim. The country in which *The Queue* was written has vanished, and with it the particular phenomenon it describes. In the 1980s Vladimir Sorokin was a cult figure in Moscow's literary underground, part of a group of self-styled conceptualists whose experimental work could be published only abroad or in samizdat. Today he is one of the best-known writers in Russia—author of some twenty novels and plays, several film scripts, and an opera libretto commissioned by the Bolshoi. Two of the films have won prestigious international prizes, and in 2001 Sorokin received the Andrei Belyi award for contributions to Russian literature.

Nevertheless, Sorokin remains a deeply controversial figure, admired and reviled in equal measure. In 2002, at the instigation of a pro-Putin youth group called Moving Together, he was notoriously prosecuted for "distributing pornography"— the first time any such charge had been brought since censorship was abolished in post-Soviet Russia.† The chosen *causus delicti* was a passage from the 1999 novel *Blue Lard*, in which

---

* Readers International, New York and London, 1988. The original translation was made from the first edition of the book, published in Russian by Syntaxe, Paris, 1985. The present version is based on Sorokin's slightly revised text, published by I. P. Bogat, Moscow, 2007.

† For an account of the case, see Jamey Gambrell, "Russia's New Vigilantes," *The New York Review of Books*, January 16, 2003.

Khrushchev and Stalin are described whispering endearments to each other while engaging in anal sex. In truth, however, any number of passages from Sorokin's work might have served the purpose. Ever since he started writing Sorokin has been breaking taboos, introducing scenes of ritualized sex and violence, rape, incest, cannibalism, and coprophilia into the most sacrosanct settings and routinely violating the decorum of every literary style he sets out to mimic and unravel. A brilliant ventriloquist, Sorokin in recent years has shifted seamlessly from the mass language of the bygone Soviet era to that of the new: from subversive pastiches of Russian and Soviet classics to bizarre renderings of modern pulp fiction. Still, the underlying themes remain: on the one hand, entrapment in a society steeped in violence, brutality, hypocrisy, and sham; on the other, the search by "unfortunates" for an exit—salvation.

These themes are already manifest in *The Queue*, Sorokin's first novel, which pits a hapless individual against one of the strangest excrescences of the Soviet era: the monster queue. Yet in many ways *The Queue* is the exception among Sorokin's works. For a start, it grants the reader an unequivocally happy ending: in the best traditions of Russian literature the hero finds salvation, and his heart's desire, in the arms of a woman. Moreover, no one is raped, mutilated, or eaten on the way; the sex is friendly, the violence confined. And in comparison with the baroque plots of the later works, the story of *The Queue* has a kind of Mozartian simplicity.

That one can speak of a story at all is testament to Sorokin's virtuosity, for in *The Queue* he denies himself every narrative prop. With no narrator, no description, no formally identified characters, the novel consists entirely of unattributed utterances —the words, grunts, and sighs of the people caught up in a gigantic line, somewhere in a suburb of Moscow in the late 1970s. At first, the scraps of conversation appear little more than random noise. But in a moment distinct voices begin to emerge, and presently, like a developing photo, the entire, slow-shifting scene begins to take shape: the summer heat, the boredom, the din of megaphones. There's that frazzled mother again, perpetually scolding her little boy ("Volodya, put on your hat!"); there's the woman at the *kvass* barrel, dishing out her lifesaving beverage; there's the drunkard pissing against the wall, the stray cat mewing, the Beatles playing from an open window; and here in the midst of it all is Vadim Alekseev, failed journalist, idle vacationer, and unmistakably the hero of the piece. We watch him patiently cajole the arch, humorless Lena; see how she (faithless hussy!) discards him in favor of a more attractive prospect (a writer, of course) who picks her up in the canteen; watch with dismay as Vadim, unaware of her betrayal, falls in with a bunch of ne'er-do-wells and drinks himself unconscious; then, just as all goes dark (a dreadful thunderstorm) witness his miraculous resurrection at the hands of gentle Lyuda, provider of all things good and nourishing: warmth, shelter, poetry, fried potatoes, unlimited sex—and (who knows) perhaps the very items Vadim has been queuing for.

If part of the pleasure in reading *The Queue* lies in picking out this "melody" (and the numerous sub-melodies along the way), a related satisfaction comes simply from the novel's perfect—sometimes pitiless—realism. Even the excruciating roll call exerts a certain fascination (all those Russian, Jewish, Lithuanian, Ukrainian names that had to be invented). Moreover, with the passage of time (as Sorokin's afterword suggests) the experience of recognition is inevitably inflected with a kind of nostalgia. Nowhere does one feel this more keenly than in the evocation of Lyuda's tiny apartment, Vadim's refuge from the queue, with its glassed-in veranda, accommodating bathtub, china knickknacks, tea caddy, frying pan, and handy bottle of Hungarian Vermouth. In an interview in 1987 Sorokin contrasted the "cosy mini-world of the apartment" with the harsh ideologized space of the street: shut the stout leather-lined door in those days and ideology vanished.* Today even the best-lined doors offer little proof against the anxieties and exigencies of the post-Soviet age.

A novel so firmly anchored in time and place, and which relies entirely on colloquial speech, poses certain problems to the translator. Nowhere else in the world has the queue, as a phenomenon, developed to such extraordinary lengths, accrued such a wealth of ritual and lore, or acquired such potency as a symbol. The people in Sorokin's queue speak in laconic, ritualized utterances perfectly suited to their survival in the context, but not always easily transferable to English. Still, what one might call the "deep grammar" of the book—to want, to wait, to be thwarted, to get—is universal; it forms the basis for our compassion. Certain types, too, seem to crop up everywhere: that nauseating guy bragging about his sexual prowess, or those elderly folk waxing lyrical about the good old days—haven't we heard them somewhere before? Because I grew up in London, the English I hear these Russians speak is the English you might hear among a crowd of people waiting eagerly to see the queen (some of them have been camping out all night in the rain), or waiting to grab the best furs when Selfridges opens for the winter sales, or standing on a tube platform when all the trains have been canceled and no one can hear what the loudspeaker is saying. I trust their curses and exclamations, though rendered in "English English," will be understandable to readers on both sides of the Atlantic.

—SALLY LAIRD

* Sally Laird, *Voices of Russian Literature* (Oxford University Press, 1999), p. 148.

THE QUEUE

— Comrade, who's last in the queue?
— I am, I think, but there was a woman in a blue coat after me.
— So I'm after her?
— Yes, she'll be back in a moment. You stand behind me in the meantime.
— You're staying here then, are you?
— Yes.
— I just wanted to nip off for a moment—I'll literally be a minute.
— I think you better wait for her, 'cos what can I say if somebody else comes along? If you hold on a moment, she said she wouldn't be long.
— Okay then, I'll wait. You been queuing long?
— Not really...
— How many are they giving per person, d'you know?
— God knows...haven't even asked. Do you know how many each they're giving out?
— Don't know about today. I heard yesterday it was two each.
— Two?
— Uh-huh. First it was four each, then two.
— Not a lot, huh! Hardly worth waiting, really...
— You should get into two queues at once. Those guys from out of town have got places in three different queues.
— Three each?
— Uh-huh.

— Then we're going to be here all day!

— Nah, don't worry. Service is very quick here.

— I'm not so sure. We haven't budged an inch...

— That's 'cos those people have just come back again. Whole bunch of them—they'd all gone off for a while.

— They all go off and then all pile in at once.

— Don't worry, things'll move quickly now.

— You don't know how many they're giving each?

— Three each, I'm told.

— That's a bit more like it. Over at Savelovsky it's just one each as a rule.

— Well there's not much point over there giving more, is there. Folks from out of town take the whole lot anyway...

— So was there as big a queue yesterday, then?

— Almost.

— And were you queuing yesterday as well?

— Uh-huh.

— For very long?

— Oh, not very...

— And they're not too crushed?

— Well, they were okay to start with, but by the end they were handing out any old stuff.

— Be the same thing today, no doubt. All the good ones'll be taken, and we'll be left with the junk.

— They're all much of a muchness, I had a look.

— Really?

— Yes, they withdraw the ones that aren't any good.

— Come off it, withdraw them? A likely story!

— They're obliged to report what's damaged and send it back.

— Obliged my foot! Make a fortune out of them, that's what they do...

— Well, we'll see, no need to argue...

— That lady's come back. You're behind her.

— The tall one?

— Yes.

— So I'm after you, am I?

— Seems so. I'm behind this citizen here.

— Then I'm after you.

— And I'm after you.

— Right, and you're after me, okay. So d'you mind if I just go off for a minute now?

— Go ahead.

— I'll only be a minute, I'm just getting my laundry... it's just round the corner.

— Are they open till six today?

— I think so, yes...

— I'll dash over there later then...

— Have they got any cabbages yet, d'you know?

— No, there's a queue for oranges, but they haven't got any cabbages.

— It's too early for cabbages, no point getting them yet.

— They were selling the new ones on Leninsky, and they were perfectly alright.

— Come off it! Just a bunch of leaves.

— Fresh young cabbage is very good for you.

— Look how they're pushing in up there, absolutely shameless. Why d'you let them in, citizen? Are we supposed to stand here all day?! Just pushing in, look at them!

— They had places in the queue, they just went off for a bit...

— Had places indeed! They had nothing of the sort.

— Yes we did, there's no need to shout.

— You never had places at all! I've been queuing here since morning.

— They did have, I saw...

— They get their places and then go off for half the day.

— I reckon they never even had places. I never saw them.

— Yes they did.

— We did, we did...

— Calm down, they did!

— Calm down yourself!

— Okay okay, no need to start yelling about nothing. These people were standing in the queue, and then they went off somewhere. Nothing to get upset about . . .

— She's taking ages to serve . . .

— Can you see?

— Just.

— That red-head's damn slow. She was so sluggish yesterday, more dead than alive.

— Is there really just the one of them?

— Two.

— I can't even see . . .

— Come over here, you can see from here.

— Oh yes. Two of them. That one looks a bit snappier.

— The dark one's quicker with the service.

— They're both doing their best, it's just there are so many people.

— There always are.

— And those people are taking an age to pick and choose.

— So . . . we haven't moved an inch . . .

— Don't worry, we'll be moving faster now.

— I only hope they let us have three each.

— They will.

— So long as we make it in time . . .

— There'll be plenty for us.

— When did they finish yesterday, d'you know?

— I don't remember—I left . . .

— Excuse me, am I after you?

— No, you're in front.

— Oh, yes! I'm after you.

— That's right.

— I only just made it to the laundry.

— Why, are they closing early today?

— They wouldn't let anyone in after me.

— Really...

— Tell me, you didn't get your butter over there, did you?

— No, in the centre.

— This morning they had some over there at three fifty, but there isn't any left now.

— They sometimes have it in the afternoon...

— Sometimes they get some in the morning too... What are they up to now? Chatting away for hours on end!

— Another bunch of Georgians... hey look, look, they're just barging straight in! Hey, lady! Don't let them in! What a nerve!

— They'll take twenty each and then re-sell them.

— 'Course they will... There, that's the way to do it. Get rid of that one too!

— What's that laundry like, any good?

— Not bad, I think, but a bit slow.

— Take ages, do they?

— Yes, a month.

— That's a fair time. But the things don't get lost?

— Not as a rule.

— That's okay, then... Look, another Georgian's turned up...

— I've never yet seen a Georgian stand in a queue.

— I think I'll be off, you know...

— Are you leaving?

— Yes. It's past two, and we haven't yet moved...

— Who's last, are you?

— Yes, I am.

— You come in here, my girl. The guy who was here just left, you can take his place.

— Thanks.

— No thanks to me, it's him that's done you a favour. Did you get your carnations at the market?

— No, in a shop.

— What, that one over on the right?

— Yes.

— Such nice ones too. You're a lucky girl.

— All the ones they've got there are nice and big.

— I've never got any that size, so you must be lucky.

— It had nothing to do with me.

— Of course it did. Nice girls are always lucky.

— What nonsense ... have you been queuing long?

— Not very.

— Slow going, is it?

— It'll go a whole lot faster now.

— Why's that?

— 'Cos you've arrived.

— Oh, for heaven's sake! Think you can take all comers, don't you, clever dick.

— No need to be rude. I do know a thing or two.

— Been to college then, have you?

— I have.

— Where?

— Oh, here, there and everywhere.

— Learned a little bit of everything, is that it?

— That's right. So tell me now, what's your name?

— And why should I tell you?

— Because I need to know, that's why.

— You don't need to know, and I'm not telling.

— Go on, don't be mean, tell me.

— But why should I tell you?

— Why shouldn't you? Is it such a big deal?

— No, no ... If you have to know, my name's Lena.

— And mine's Vadim.

— And so?

— So nothing. Just that I can breathe again now.

— Honestly!

— Honestly what?

— Nothing.

— What d'you mean, nothing?

— Could you calm down a bit now, young man!

— Why, I'm not disturbing you, am I?

— Stands there going bla bla bla, bla bla bla. How about a bit of quiet now?

— You could keep quiet yourself.

— There you go again, why don't you keep quiet.

— You keep quiet. No need to get upset.

— You're the one that's upset.

— Well, you really...you're not by any chance at the Textiles Institute, are you, Lena?

— Well guessed.

— Didn't take much guessing. A, the Textiles is just round the corner, and B, you're a nice girl. It all adds up.

— Got it all worked out, haven't you...Hey, look at them pushing in...

— Hey, take it easy now, what are you shoving for?

— I'm not the one shoving, it's those people in front!

— This is crazy. Christ, look where you're going...

— Ow, they're squashing us!...Hey, you! Watch what you're doing, will you!

— It wasn't me!

— What is all this? Why are we moving backwards?

— What's happening up there?

— Can't see a thing...

— Hey, citizen, what's going on there?

— They're straightening out the queue.

— Of all the crazy...I was standing here an hour ago...what's all this about...

— A bit more now, how on earth can we...

— Still, it'll move faster this way...

— I wouldn't bank on it...They keep on pushing—what are you pushing for?

— I'm not pushing, I'm just standing here.

— Has the laundry closed now, citizen?

— Yes. Like I was saying—I only just made it.

— We've missed it, then. Have to go after dinner now.

— Give me your bag, Lena.

— Don't be silly, there's no need.

— No go on, give it to me.

— But there's no need, I can hold it myself.

— Give it to me or I'll take it from you!

— Well, if you insist . . . take it by all means.

— Wow, this weighs a ton. How did you manage to carry it?

— Just did.

— But what have you got in here—dumbbells?

— Books.

— Oh, I see.

— We've just finished term.

— Congratulations! I've long since forgotten about term-times myself.

— So where did you do your studies, then?

— Moscow University.

— Lucky you. What did you study?

— History.

— That's interesting. I've always had a blank spot about history.

— That's 'cos you never studied it seriously.

— Maybe. Must be really interesting though—all those tsars, and wars, and the ice age and stuff like that . . . You don't know what kind they are, do you, Vadim?

— Yugoslav, apparently.

— Czech.

— Are you sure?

— I was queuing for them yesterday.

— There we are then, Lena—they're Czech. Don't mind if I call you '*tu*'?

— Do as you please. It was a good idea they had to straighten out the queue. It's going faster now.

— Seems to be.

— You wouldn't have a cigarette would you, mate?

— Sure. Help yourself.

— Thanks.

— D'you know if there's been a big delivery?

— No, that I wouldn't know.

— But there'll be enough for us, will there?

— Ask me another, old man.

— They've got some new potatoes...

— Probably from the shop over there...

— I've just been there. They didn't have any.

— Must be from the market.

— Must be. Watch out, mate, you've dropped your...

— Ooh, thanks...

— Have to take it back to the dry cleaner's!

— Nah, nothing to worry about...just a spot of dust...

— Listen, d'you live near here?

— In that apartment block over there.

— There isn't a hairdresser's nearby, is there?

— Why, d'you want to ruin your lovely hair?

— None of your business—hey, why are you pushing...

— Don't push.

— I'm not pushing. It's them up there.

— Stamping on people's feet...So there is a hairdresser's, is there?

— Uh-huh. Not all that near, but there is one. How to explain...you go up half a block, then turn right. It's a tiny little side street.

— What's it called?

— I don't remember...something-or-other alley...

— So, straight and then right?

— Yes... But why don't I come with you, otherwise you'll get lost.

— No no, there's no need, I'll find it.

— Come on, let's go.

— What about the queue?

— You don't think we'll miss it, do you?! Must be joking! Look how many have joined on behind us.

— Goodness! Can't even see the end of it.

— If you'll excuse us, we'll just be gone for half an hour or so, okay?

— Please yourselves.

— Come on then.

— Yes, ye-es... No one wants to stand and wait.

— Well, what d'you expect. Young folks... it's dull for them.

— While it's not dull for us, is that it?

— They run off to do what they want, and we're left to stew in the heat.

— Yes, it's baking... It was sort of cloudy before, but now look at it!

— What did they say it would be today?

— Twenty-three.

— Must be twenty-five by now.

— No no, can't be as high as that...

— I'm telling you, it's twenty-five.

— It only seems that hot 'cos it's so humid... there isn't a breath of wind.

— Funny, the poplars are swaying a bit, but you can't feel any breeze. No freshness in the air.

— That's how it is in town— never gets really fresh. You need a river and fields if you want fresh air. Here all you've got is dust and asphalt...

— The building up there gives a bit of shade.

— Yes, but we've got to get there first... we're not moving at all...

— We are, we are. Look, that bin's behind us now.

— Always was behind us, seems to me.

— No, come on, it wasn't.

— I think I'll go and get an ice cream ... won't be a minute ...

— You couldn't get one for me, could you? Twenty-eight kopeks ... here, let me give it to you ...

— Okay.

— You don't mind?

— There's probably a queue for the ice cream too.

— A small one, but not too bad.

— How can she wear that coat! Makes your head spin to look at her!

— I know ...

— Some people just feel cold, you know. There's an illness like that.

— You don't know, do you, what colour they are?

— All different ones.

— I gather they're mainly light brown.

— Aren't there any dark ones?

— Yes, there are dark ones too.

— That's good.

— I must say I'd prefer a darker one.

— Well, it's just the luck of the draw. They've got either the one or the other.

— This is it. Depending what comes in, that's what we'll get.

— Excuse me, was I after you?

— No, you're after that lady.

— Oh yes, that's right.

— They go wandering off and then have to go asking every-one ...

— What's going on there ... can't make out ...

— What d'you mean?

— Over there look ... what's she yelling about?

— Someone's pushed in ...

— And who's that...
— Yeah, you're right...
— Stupid fool!
— They should be chucked out, they should.
— Just wasting our time.
— Why don't you put your bag down here. Handy place—on this ledge, look.
— Ah, right.
— I'm told they were on sale downtown yesterday.
— Well there's no way you'd get in there.
— All of them dark brown, mind you.
— Really?
— Uh-huh.
— Sometimes they decide to bring out the goods, but there's no telling where it'll be.
— It was out of the blue here too...I only just made it...
— My neighbour it was told me, yesterday.
— Probably heard about it from one of the salesgirls?
— I don't know.
— God, why do they have to take such an age...
— He's trying to push in again. What a nerve!
— They just shouldn't let him do it.
— Great hulking fellow too, and look what he's doing.
— Your bag's leaking.
— Whoops, thanks! It's the meat...oh my God...Fedya, take it...
— Here, give it to me, quick...
— But take it by the handle! What the hell are you...
— Get it out from under the bread...here...
— You take it.
— Volodya.
— Hold it the right way up, what are you doing!
— No need to yell...
— Volodya!

— Are they really giving people three each?

— Looks like it.

— I'm after you, aren't I?

— That's right. After me. Didn't take too long?

— No no. Here's your change. It's a bit runny though...

— That's okay. Thanks. Whoops, I'm afraid it's going to drip everywhere.

— I was worried they'd run out.

— Why, are they running out already?

— Uh-huh.

— Volodya! What are you standing there for?! Come over here!

— Twenty-eight kopeks, was it?

— Yeah, they just had these and the ten-kopek ones.

— Phew... this heat...

— Just a bit further and we'll be in the shade. And then it's not far at all.

— Seryozha, take it...

— Why don't I hang it on the pram.

— Real parasites though... look how he's pushing in...

— Someone ought to go and tell them. Otherwise they'll all push in and there won't be any left for us.

— You're right.

— Just shameless.

— And that woman with him. The greedy so-and-so.

— What's going on, for goodness sake...

— You're dripping it on your trousers, friend.

— Oh no, it's melting... damn the thing... I'm all covered in it...

— Zina, you lean against the wall, take a rest...

— She's alright, she's a big girl, she can stand like everyone else. You can stand alright, can't you, eh?

— Yes.

— That's right, good girl.

— Did you get your butter at *Cheese*?

— No, in that place over there.

— But they're out of it there.

— I got it this morning.

— Aah!... Yes, it has gone rather soft, hasn't it, a bit squashed...

— I'll never make it home today! What a joke!

— Same here. I left home at twelve, so I've managed to get in three different queues already.

— So now. At least one policeman's arrived.

— They ought to give just two each, otherwise there won't be enough for everyone.

— There'll be enough, there'll be enough. They don't deal in piddling quantities.

— D'you know what kind of lining they've got?

— Flimsy stuff.

— Not very warm?

— Nah.

— Too bad!

— What's the problem?

— Nothing...

— Volodya, don't run around here. A car might come up.

— Don't run around, boy. It's a turning here—very dangerous.

— You just stand here.

— Mum, I'm thirsty.

— Stand still, don't be silly.

— But Mum, I'm thirsty!

— Did you hear what I said! Give me your hand! Stand next to me.

— He just came and went. What kind of policeman's that...

— They don't overdo it, don't you worry.

— They ought at least to try and keep order.

— Those wogs've pushed in again. Disgusting.

— Shouldn't be allowed in!

— They creep in everywhere.

— Mum! I'm thirsty!

— Shut up!
— You ought to take the boy for a drink. There are some machines nearby.
— Where?
— Just a bit past *Synthetics.*
— Thanks. I'll go for a minute then . . . Come on, Volodya . . .
— Mum, have we got three kopeks?
— Yes, yes . . . come on now . . . so, I'm after you, aren't I . . .
— Seryozha, put it down by the wall.
— Phew, that's better, we're in the shade now . . .
— We've made it! Hurrah . . .
— Right, I think we're after you, aren't we?
— Yes, yes.
— Stand here, Lena.
— We don't seem to have moved much . . .
— What d'you mean, not much! We're already past that building.
— It's nice here.
— Yeah. It's better in the shade. So, have they dried?
— Yes. Look what a lovely colour.
— I don't understand about painting your nails.
— Why not?
— I don't know.
— What, you don't think it makes any difference?
— Well, no, I can't see the difference between one polish and the next.
— But there are nasty colours and there are nice ones . . .
— Maybe, God knows.
— Anyway, it's a good hairdresser's you've got there.
— You liked them, did you?
— Uh-huh, and there weren't too many people either.
— Well, you know the way now, so whenever you want . . .
— I will . . . Listen, you don't know what kind of sole they've got?

— Synthetic, I'm told.

— Seriously! That's great!

— They're nice imported ones, I saw them.

— I couldn't get up there. Couldn't even get near.

— I saw some that a woman had got.

— Nice colour?

— Quite nice— greyish-brown.

— Suede-look?

— Uh-huh.

— Nonsense, young man. They're leather.

— Leather?

— Really?

— They can't be, I saw them myself...

— Quite right, but they only had the suede type this morning; they ran out by lunchtime. Now they're leather—dark brown.

— Oh, hell.

— And we've been standing here like idiots. I'm leaving then, Vadim...

— Hold on, hold on...

— Why hold on?

— Wait... these ones may be alright.

— Come off it, 'course they aren't.

— But why...

— You're not going to stay, are you?

— But what difference does it make if they're suede-look or leather?

— It makes a big difference to me.

— But Lena, maybe we should stay?

— No, I'm going. You stay.

— But look how close we are already! What's the point of standing all this time?

— We are pretty close...

— Why don't you stay, huh?

— No, I'm off. See you.

— I'll phone you tomorrow.

— As you like. Bye.

— Bye.

— That's today's fashion for you. The leather ones are no good any more.

— That's right...

— You couldn't give me a bit of your newspaper could you, just to fan myself a bit...

— Take the whole thing.

— Thanks.

— We seem to be moving.

— About time too.

— I'm going to go and sit down...

— Vadim.

— Lena?!

— I changed my mind. It's true, you know, what difference does it make...

— That's my girl... Here's for being good...

— Behave yourself... everyone's looking...

— So we're going to stay?! Hurrah!

— You don't know what's on at the *Stakhanovite*, do you?

— Some Italian film.

— Any good?

— Don't know.

— I wanted to go look at the poster and find out what's on, but would you believe, I couldn't get past.

— Why not?

— 'Cos our queue stretches all the way up there. That's where the end is.

— Right up at *Synthetics*?

— Uh-huh.

— Can't be.

— It can.

— That's quite something.

— And new people are joining on, that's the thing.

— Then of course it makes sense to stay.

— That's what I thought.

— And we're so near too.

— You young people are pushing me right into the wall...

— Sorry.

— So... were we after you?

— That's right. Did our hero get his drink?

— He gulped down two glasses. Stand here, don't wriggle...

— I would've drunk a third one but we didn't have the right money.

— Where would you have put a third one? You'd have burst.

— I wouldn't.

— You wouldn't?

— I wouldn't.

— A real hero.

— Excuse me, did you knit your top by hand or on a machine?

— By hand.

— It's really nice.

— Do you like it?

— Yes. The wool's so soft.

— Lena, I'm going to run off and get some ice cream.

— Sure.

— More and more people keep coming... it's crazy.

— They were here before. I saw them.

— I don't remember them somehow.

— They were here, they were here. I'm certain.

— Can't work out what's going on...

— They were here, they were here...

— Why does he have to drive straight into people... idiot...

— Couldn't pull up alongside.

— What kind of buses are they?

— I can't make out... must be chartered...

— Ooh, look at all those people...where on earth...

— Three buses...Here comes a third...

— Uh-huh...a third one too...

— Must be workers...

— No no, no way those are workers. It's a tour.

— Where would out-of-towners be going? There aren't any museums round here.

— Maybe there are.

— There aren't, I've lived here forty years.

— God, what a crowd! They crawl out in this heat...

— Hello, what's up now?

— Where are they going? Why...?

— What are they standing there for?!

— This is disgraceful!

— What are you doing, pushing in like that? Hey, you! You shout at them!

— Why are they pushing in! Damned nerve!

— Don't let them in! Who do they think they are?!

— Jerks! Look, look!

— What *is* this, honestly?! Call the police!

— You there, can you go and get the police?

— Bastards!

— Stupid louts!

— And all shoving in at once!

— Police! Call the police!

— Needs his ugly mug bashed in!

— Police!

— There he is, tell him!

— Look, look! What do they think we are?!

— But who the hell are they?!

— God knows! Must've come from out of town.

— Filthy peasants! I'd shoot the lot of them!

— What a nerve—just came and stood there!

— Go on, tell him properly! Where's he gone?

— He's over there.

— There's another two coming!

— At least the police are right here...

— The cheek of it, though!

— I've never seen such a thing!

— They just go and push right in!

— Why don't the police say something?!

— That one with the megaphone, gone to sleep has he? Policeman!

— He's about to say something.

— Can you see him?

— Yes, he's got up on a box.

— Ah, now I see...

— But what's the point talking! They should just chuck 'em out, the jerks!

— He's about to say something.

— What's the point...

— CITIZENS! CAN YOU PLEASE BE QUIET!

— We weren't making any noise...

— Why've they pushed in?

— And who the hell are they, can he explain!

— CAN YOU PLEASE BE QUIET! THESE COMRADES HAVE THE RIGHT TO RECEIVE GOODS WITHOUT QUEUING! SO PLEASE KEEP QUIET AND STAY CALM!

— Who's that?

— And who on earth are they!?

— This is disgraceful!

— What about us?!

— I REPEAT! WOULD YOU PLEASE BE QUIET AND KEEP ORDER! THE COMRADES WHO HAVE COME IN THE BUSES HAVE THE RIGHT TO BUY WITHOUT QUEUING!

— And what about us?!

— Why do they have the right?

— I also have the right!

— The sods!

— We've waited and waited and now look!

— What a disgrace!

— FOR THE THIRD TIME I REPEAT! THEY HAVE THE RIGHT TO BUY WITHOUT QUEUING! WOULD YOU PLEASE BE QUIET! KEEP ORDER! OTHERWISE YOU'LL BE TAKEN OUT OF THE QUEUE!

— So it's us they're going to take away! Idiot...

— But this is disgraceful!

— He might have said who they were!

— What are we supposed to do, stand here till evening!

— HOW MANY TIMES DO I HAVE TO REPEAT! WOULD YOU PLEASE BE QUIET!

— We've waited and waited...

— I'm going, Zina...

— Look, I really don't understand, why do we have to let them in?

— They just came and stood there...

— I'm going too.

— MOVE ASIDE AND LET THE COMRADES IN! THERE'S ENOUGH FOR EVERYONE! AND NO NEED TO MAKE A NOISE! PLEASE KEEP ORDER! MOVE BACK!

— What, now we're supposed to move back?

— God...

— Stop *pushing*!

— I'm not pushing, it's someone in front...

— No need to rush...

— MOVE BACK! MOVE BACK! ALL TOGETHER!

— But where've they come from, that's what I'd like to know?

— Probably some trade union conference or other...

— Here we are, right back where we were before...

— Watch where you're going, comrade...for goodness sake, what an elephant...

— Is it my fault? Those people there are shoving...

— Was I behind you?

— I think so.

— Where's the woman gone?

— She's left. Decided not to stay.

— Aaah...I see...You know it turns out they're not Czech.

— What are they then?

— Swedish.

— Really?

— You're joking?

— I hope there's enough!

— D'you hear that, Petya, they're Swedish.

— I'm staying then.

— What, have they just brought them in?

— Uh-huh. Just now. I was up at the counter.

— Lots of them?

— I don't know. Looks like it. And they're just giving out one each.

— That's good, otherwise those greedy guts'd grab the lot.

— You don't know who they are, do you?

— Haven't the faintest. They're from somewhere out of town.

— We were standing in this place an hour ago...

— Two more assistants have turned up. Should go more quickly now.

— That'd be good.

— Lena, did you hear that, they're Swedish?

— I know. Stand by the wall, I'll lean on you.

— Okay, there we are...comfy now?

— Fine.

— You don't know what make they are?

— Couldn't say.

— Pity...

— What colour are they?

— Regular dark blue.

— Are they serving quickly?

— Yes, there are four of them now.

— CITIZENS! KEEP OFF THE ROAD! KEEP AWAY! STAND NEARER THE BUILDINGS, NEARER!

— Now he's going to be trumpeting all day...

— He's got his little toy.

— Are we playing Kiev today, d'you know?

— Yes.

— I hope we make it in time...

— We will.

— I doubt it...

— We will, we will.

— They had American ones at GUM last week.

— They don't often bring those out.

— The Swedish ones are even better. So nice and soft...

— Still, a label's a label...

— Why run after a label? If they're comfortable and look nice that's the main thing.

— Well, obviously...

— Could I have a peek at your magazine?

— Take it.

— If you like I can give you the *Evening News*.

— Alright.

— Am I squashing your shoulder, Atlas?

— Relax, relax...

— YOU MUSTN'T JOSTLE, COMRADES! OR I'LL HAVE YOU TAKEN AWAY!

— Should be taken away yourself, asshole...

— Out in the sun again. It was so lovely in the shade...

— It'll go quickly now.

— Oooooaaaaah... God, standing such a long time...

— Volodya, put on your hat!

— But I'm hot!

— Put it on, you'll get a headache.

— Oh dear...I really dropped off...crazy...

— Never mind, have a nice sleep.

— Is there anything there about today's chess?

— Let's have a look...I don't think so.

— 'Cos there's some tournament going on...

— The interzonal in Spain.

— But what a mess we made in the soccer, eh?

— If it weren't for Dasaev it would've been even worse.

— That's right. He did some great saves.

— Zoff did a beauty when they were playing Brazil.

— Yes, he's a good goalie too...

— A real veteran, but the way he goes after them. How about
an ice cream...

— It's closed already.

— You sure?

— Yes.

— Just look at that...

— He's used to shoving, fucking peasant...

— Volodya, do you want a tomato?

— It's warm, Mum...

— What's wrong, didn't you have enough to drink?

— Yes. Mum, can I go over there and play?

— Where? There are cars there.

— No, over there.

— Alright, off you go, only not too far!

— You've got pretty hair...

— Leave off!

— Seriously. Flaxen hair. Debussy wrote a prelude, you know.
That's what it's called. *The Girl with the Flaxen Hair.*

— It wasn't about me.

— It was about you...about you...so soft...

— Vadim...what are you up to...really, not here...

— Should we sit over there a while?

— Okay.

— We're just going off for a minute, is that alright?

— Go ahead.

— You don't have the time, do you?

— Quarter to five.

— How time flies.

— Always toing and froing. They can't stand still.

— There we are—he barks for a while and off he goes. Doesn't do much to keep order.

— There's another pair up at the counter.

— Who the hell let that lot in? We should've all said no and had done with them.

— Easier said than done...

— Right, I was after you.

— Did you get it?

— Not a chance. But I had a drink of *kvass*.

— Where?

— Not far from here. Just round the corner and a couple of buildings down.

— Seriously?

— Uh-huh, and there aren't too many people.

— I'm going to go.

— Us too, comrades.

— We'll go first, and then you.

— Oh come on, all the *kvass* will be finished.

— What's all the fuss about, there'll be plenty left.

— Off they run, and we just get to stand here. No, really. Everyone keeps going off, and we stand here like stumps.

— You're right. Why don't we go first, then you.

— You're young, you can hold on for a bit.

— That's not the point...

— Listen, maybe we can all go somehow?

— How d'you mean?

— Go in a big group.

— Then the people at the back'll start yelling...

— And won't let us back in...

— Come off it, sure they will. Still, it's a bit awkward...

— Look, comrades, how about shifting the whole queue over there?

— What d'you mean?

— Just shift it! It's just round the corner! If we bend the queue, everyone can have a drink. That way there's no fuss and we stay in the right order.

— Great idea! Here's somebody with a head on his shoulders! Comrades, let's move!

— What's all this?

— There's a *kvass* barrel over there.

— Really?

— Our friend here's just had some. Not a soul there. Let's move and we can all wet our whistle.

— He's got a point, you know. That way we won't all be running to and fro.

— But what about the people up front?

— Well, there won't be enough for everyone, clearly.

— Fair enough, then, let's get moving.

— Maybe there'll be some shade there.

— We're moving, citizens!

— But where exactly round the corner? I can't see anything.

— There, behind that building.

— That one over there?

— No, the next one.

— Hey, no need to push though.

— Bend round there, comrades, don't just stand there.

— It's quite a long way, mind you...

— And it's in the shade too.

— They're all rushing off in a herd...where are you off to?

— We're going to get in a muddle like this.

— No we won't, don't worry.

— Volodya, come here!

— You've dropped your newspaper...

— Damn...can't get it now...

— Along the wall, along the wall, comrades.

— There's no need to shove me, sweetheart.

— Who's shoving you! You're shoving yourself!

— Behind that house?

— That's right.

— It's nice and cool here.

— Volodya! Give me your hand!

— Shit! Why the fuck d'you have to stamp on my foot?

— Sorry, mate.

— Hurry up, Lena.

— Look, there really is a barrel.

— No need to rush...

— Right here along the wall then.

— I'm after you.

— Phew...quite a queue.

— We can bend round here.

— Where are you good people off to?

— We've come to see you, mother, to quench our thirst.

— Goodness, what a lot of you! Where have you all come from?

— Over there...

— Bend round, bend round here, comrades...

— Is the *kvass* cold?

— Of course.

— Give us a big one, mother.

— I'll deal with the old queue first and then I'll come to you lot.

— There are just the two of them...

— Three litres...

— Move round the barrel now, bend round.

— Was I behind you?

29

— No, after that man there.

— Thirty-six ... next?

— Two large.

— Twelve ... haven't you got any change ...

— I'll just have a look ... ah, here ... there we are ...

— That's more like it. Thank you. Next?

— One large.

— There ... four kopeks ...

— Whoops, it's splashing ...

— Move away from here now. It's all wet, look.

— One large.

— That's nine ... there you are ... next?

— Two large and one small.

— Fifteen ... pass me back that mug ...

— A small one, please.

— One small—there you go ...

— One large ...

— I need change, comrades ...

— Here's ten.

— Four ...

— One large.

— Forty-four ...

— Same again ... there's the exact change.

— Right ... next?

— A large.

— One rouble ... a rouble ... take it ...

— One small ... I've got the exact ...

— Move aside now ... over to the left, next?

— Two small.

— Two ...

— One large ...

— Hold on.

— Thanks, very nice *kvass*.

— Give back your mugs.

— Right . . . ten kopeks . . .

— One small.

— Three . . .

— A large and a small.

— Twenty . . . eleven . . .

— Here, Misha . . .

— Your mugs, your mugs, please!

— A large.

— Six . . . have you got one kopek?

— Yes . . . there you are . . .

— Give me the biggest you've got.

— One large . . . don't lean so hard . . .

— Mum, I wanna big one.

— A small one for us, please.

— Oh, Mum!

— Twelve kopeks . . . take it . . .

— Don't hog the mugs, give them back here!

— Large.

— Ten. Six.

— Small.

— Hold on.

— There's yours.

— One large.

— I remember. There's your rouble . . .

— One small.

— There.

— And one for me.

— Damn . . .

— Never mind . . . Quite nice to have a sprinkling . . .

— Large.

— That's for you then . . . there . . .

— And another.

— Mugs!

— Can you pass it back. Thanks.

— Next?

— I'd like ... I'd like ...

— What?

— A large one.

— Why not say so ...

— You go over there.

— That's yours. Next?

— He's getting it.

— Next?

— Two large.

— Right ... damn ... why's it dripping ...

— Cracked ...

— Give it here. There.

— Same for me.

— There you go. Nine.

— One small.

— Shit ...

— Like a fountain ...

— I'll say!

— Thanks.

— What do you want, lovey?

— A small one.

— And you, dear?

— A big one.

— You won't burst?

— Nope.

— Three ... six ... six ...

— Thanks.

— You're welcome.

— A big one. And one for him.

— The same?

— Yep.

— What's that you're giving me?

— Ooh, sorry. There you are.

— That's more like it ... Mugs!

— Thanks ... there's your mug, now.

— Right ... let's think, give me ...

— That's mine.

— Right ... twenty-two change ...

— That's good ...

— Don't spill it on your trousers.

— One large.

— There. One large ... Four.

— Put it here.

— Next?

— One large.

— You don't have a kopek?

— I'll have a look ...

— Do that. A large for you? Next?

— Three large.

— There's one kopek.

— Right. Three large ...

— I've only got a fiver.

— Okay, we'll manage.

— Thanks.

— That's four roubles.

— One small.

— Next?

— Small?

— There ... three ... next?

— Lena, are you going to have a small one?

— Yes.

— One large and one small.

— One kopek ... take it ...

— Thanks.

— Let's move away a bit ... mmmm ... nice and cold ...

— Yes ... aah ... this is the proper stuff, not too diluted.

— Ooh ... I've never drunk it in one gulp. Thanks.

— Like some more?

— Goodness no, you drink up.

— Aah . . . great stuff. Thanks. So, where were we?

— Right down there. Miles away. What a joke!

— Never mind. Nothing to be done about it. Let's go.

— That was a great idea that guy had to bend the queue round here.

— Pure genius.

— My mouth had completely dried up. Made all the difference.

— Life worth living again, is it?

— That's right. Were we after you?

— Yes.

— So how did you like the *kvass*?

— Not bad. And you?

— Great. Specially because it was out of the blue. You stand there for hours in the heat and suddenly you get a touch of shade and some nice cold *kvass*.

— Seems to me it doesn't make much difference where you stand.

— Well, it's a bit better in the shade though.

— It is.

— Really hidden herself in the underbrush hasn't she? Must be known and loved by all the locals.

— That's it . . .

— She'll have a hard time now, though. Be sold out in an hour.

— That's right.

— Vadik, give me a coin, I'm going to make a phone call.

— A coin . . . wait a sec . . . here, two kopeks.

— People keep on looking to see what there's such a big queue for, and it's all for *kvass*! What a farce!

— And they can't understand why everyone stays queuing up afterwards!

— Here we go now . . . look at that . . .

— He just broke it by mistake.

— Must be drunk. Can't keep hold of his mug.

— He's not drunk.

— Yes he is.

— No he's not. Just dazed by the heat.

— You've dropped something, citizen.

— Oh, thanks.

— Look at that. Might have been run over.

— Completely reckless.

— It's because of these old ladies that most accidents happen.

— They deserve to be run over. If someone'd hurtled round the corner just now, what could they have done? Would've gone straight into us!

— There was an accident like that last month on Lenin Avenue. A woman dashed across the road, a truck jumps out of Lomonosov Street, and she flies straight in front of the wheels. Well, he swerves—young fellow it was—and ploughs straight into a bus stop. Three dead and another three taken to hospital in serious condition.

— What about the woman?

— Nowhere to be seen!

— God, of all the lowdown things! And people died because of her.

— Yes, and the guy'll probably be in for something too.

— That's just it. Don't make much attempt to look into things here, do we?

— That's not fair now. They'll look into it.

— Ah, come on! Look into it! The police go round killing and stealing themselves. There was that trial, remember, when they robbed people in the metro.

— Lots of people were shot for that, I heard.

— A hundred.

— Sixty it was, not a hundred.

— A hundred's what I heard.

— Sixty.

— Makes no difference in any case. They just carry on regardless, the swine. I heard they're recruiting convicts now.

— They've just had a pay rise too.

— And they don't do a damned thing...

— So, did you make your phone call?

— I made my phone call alright, but you'll never guess what! Two more busloads have arrived, it's madness!

— The same bunch?

— Uh-huh!

— Well, they've got a real nerve!

— Turns out they're some sort of delegation—front-line workers from the regions.

— Jerks!

— Why couldn't they cart them off somewhere else?

— That's really pushing it!

— Yes... but you'll never guess what, they've brought a truckload of American ones in too!

— You're kidding!

— No, honestly.

— Bastards! There'll never be enough for us.

— I heard they're going to bring some more, so there may be enough.

— Sure there will.

— The main thing is they're going to carry on selling late today, apparently. Got to get rid of the stuff quickly for some reason.

— You've been up to the counter, have you, love?

— No, I heard what the policeman was saying over the megaphone.

— What does late mean?

— Till eleven, I think.

— But honestly—American ones?

— Yep.

— Why'd they suddenly think of that when the day's almost over?

— God knows.

— Was it a big crowd turned up?

— Hard to say.

— Front-line workers, I'll be damned. Don't do a fucking lick of work—just wait for the students to do it all. That's why there's no potatoes anywhere to be had.

— What make are they, d'you know?

— Super Rifles, I heard.

— Great. Pity there probably won't be enough.

— Maybe there will be.

— As if those peasants understood the difference between Super Rifles and their own backsides! They don't know a damn thing. All they need is a bagful of oranges and a lump of sausage. Skunks...

— Can't go anywhere in Moscow now. Every place is packed downtown, and it's just the same here.

— Careful, Lena...

— Uh-huh...

— Here we go again!

— What, are we moving backwards again?

— 'Course we are. A load more came along, didn't they, so we've got to move.

— Jesus...

— Maybe it'd be better to go round the bend instead of backwards?

— That's true, quite right. Let's move into the side street there.

— Good idea. Otherwise we'll be back at that barrel.

— Okay comrades, let's bend around into the side street.

— Let's...

— Better, of course, than milling around here...

— We're turning, turning...

— Move left, folks! Turn into the side street!

— Excuse me, did I get this from you?

— Yes.

— Thanks very much.

— You're welcome... So, shall we turn then?

— Bend round, bend round...

— Hurry up, Lenka.

— Look how they're shoving over there...

— D'you know for sure they're Super Rifles?

— Quite sure. Why?

— Can't believe it...

— Why not? They've got no reason to lie about it.

— That's true.

— It's nice here. I love these little side streets.

— Lovely and quiet, eh?

— Yeah, and it's cooler here.

— Look, a Mercedes.

— Whose can that be, I wonder?

— Looks like a Soviet number plate. Not a diplomat then.

— Must cost a bomb.

— Yeah, I should think so.

— Volodya! Put it back!

— The poplars have grown really big here...

— No one to prune them. On the main road they lop off all the tops.

— I'd love to live in a place like this. I love these two-storey buildings.

— A tower block for me.

— Why on earth?

— No noise.

— God, fancy living in a skyscraper...

— It's great. I sometimes go to my friend's place—it's a real treat. No sounds, no smells. Where I live there's a shop backing onto the yard—whole place reeks of fish. And kids running around making a racket.

— I'm not bothered by noise.

— That's what you say now. I can only work when it's really quiet.

— Why, are you writing something?

— Editing articles.

— What kind of articles?

— Historical. Well, various subjects.

— Like what?

— Well, the last one was called—hold on, let me think—oh— something about the migration of the southern Slavs.

— I wouldn't be able to make head or tail of that.

— It's all quite straightforward.

— For you.

— Come over here, you'll be more comfy.

— Can you pull me off a leaf?

— What, one of these?

— Uh-huh. I'll stick it on my nose.

— You look like Mickey Mouse now.

— Mickey Mouse yourself.

— Volodya! Where are you?

— Hold out your palm, Mickey Mouse.

— Why?

— Hold it out and I'll swat you.

— There.

— Bop!

— Nya-nya, missed me!

— Once more.

— There.

— Bop! Gottcha.

— You don't have to thrash me! Your turn now...

— Volodya!

— Oop!
— Nah!
— Bop!
— Missed!
— Bungler!
— I'm here, Mum.
— Whack! That's the way to do it.
— Why don't you answer me? Do I have to shout?
— Hold yours out.
— No, go on slybooots, you do it . . .
— Bop!
— There you go!
— Stop jostling us, you two.
— Sorry.
— Can't stand still for a minute, can you . . . can't stop giggling, ha ha ha.
— Let them play if they want to.
— I'm going to sit on that bench.
— God, it's past seven already.
— Seriously?
— Yep. Twenty past.
— Seem to have moved a bit, though.
— They've speeded up the service, I see.
— We're going to miss the soccer. It's on in ten minutes.
— There's a better match on tomorrow. Spartak v. Dinamo.
— Straight over the fence and there you go . . .
— That's right.
— Ugh—I wish you wouldn't smoke, you men, it's hard enough to breathe as it is.
— So move away from here, that'll solve your problem.
— You could move yourself.
— Why me? You move.
— Stands there puffing like a steam engine.
— You didn't ask if they'd got all sizes, did you, Lena?

— Seems so.

— Good.

— What are they pushing for?

— I don't know. What's happening over there?

— God knows.

— Hey, lady, ask them what's going on.

— What's going on? Don't tell me another bunch have turned up...

— I'm leaving.

— What are they shoving like that for...watch out!

— We're not pushing, it's them pushing us.

— Look where you're going, will you...

— Elbowing us again.

— Come here Misha.

— You too...Go on, go on...

— What's going on then, Lena?

— It's not special buses this time. Just they've decided to straighten out the queue.

— How d'you mean?

— Put people farther apart.

— Good idea...otherwise there'll be a scrum at the counter.

— That's right. This way people'll be farther apart and the queue'll be a bit longer, but the service should be quicker.

— Should be, yes.

— Comrades, let's move along.

— Move along, move along and stand further apart...

— Let's move over there.

— Into the side road. Queue'll move more quickly if you get further apart.

— What the hell difference does it make? Same damned thing whatever we do.

— It might be quicker this way, though.

— Get all sorts pushing in otherwise, crowding us out.

— A bit further...no need to push...

— I just hope we make it . . .

— Move along just a bit . . .

— There's a real whirlpool up there . . .

— Alyosha, come over here, what are you doing . . .

— There we are, it's even cooler here.

— Look, there's a little puss.

— Come over here, Lena, we can sit down here.

— Isn't it dirty?

— Nah . . .

— Sit down.

— Juts out specially for us . . . aaah . . . that's better . . .

— It's a sort of little parapet.

— It's not a parapet, young man. The peasants call it a *zavalinka*
   . . . if you don't mind . . . oop-la . . . Have a seat, Lyuda . . .

— It's dirty, Pasha . . .

— Spread out the newspaper.

— There . . . whew . . . my poor legs are aching . . .

— Shall we sit down, Uncle Senya?

— Uh-huh . . . there we are now . . .

— Move up a bit, comrades . . .

— That's nice, we can have a little sit down.

— The sun's almost gone . . . bye-bye sun . . .

— Just about bye-bye . . . it's still pretty hot.

— American ones though, huh? What luck.

— Can't believe it somehow. You're quite sure, are you?

— Go and look for yourself.

— You wouldn't have a cigarette?

— I do somewhere . . . here . . .

— Ah . . . thanks . . . nice lighter. Where's it from?

— Swedish.

— My brother had one shaped like a broad. With her legs
   spread out, see, and when you press it, out comes the flame
   from between her hands. She'd got her hands held together
   right here, see.

— It's really heavy—take a look at that, Lena.

— Looks like a real one.

— You could give someone a fright with a gun like that. *Your money or your life...*

— Nah, you can see it's just a toy.

— Sure you can.

— Want some sausage?

— Sausage? No thanks.

— There we are, we're moving now...get up, we're going to have to shift from here.

— Move along, Lyosha.

— I told you it'd go quicker now...

— Come on, Lena! We can sit on the edge here.

— What a nice little puss. Puss, puss, puss...come here...

— Don't pick her up, she's dirty.

— Look who's talking...come here, puss.

— A stray by the look of it.

— You just don't like animals, that's all.

— Oh yeah? I used to have two dogs.

— Puss puss... *that's* it...look what a nice pussy.

— Hello, Tiddles.

— Puss wuss...haven't we got a cold little nose, eh...aren't we a sweet little puss...

— Goodness knows where she's been though.

— We don't mind, do we...Little puss...see, she wants stroking...

— There...she likes that...

— Look at her eyes...they're sparkling...

— Look out, she's shedding all over the place.

— Run along now...

— The American ones are much sturdier...

— Material's much nicer too.

— Stop rushing about, Volodya.

— She's quicker than you are, that cat.

— Leave her be, Volodya!

— Stone stays really cool even when it's this hot, doesn't it?

— Of course. The earth never really warms up in these parts. My son-in-law was lying on the ground yesterday down at the dacha and already today he's got a cough.

— In the South it's the other way round—the earth gives off heat even when it's cold.

— That's right...

— Why're they taking forever for Christ's sake!

— Must be tired.

— We're all tired. But they get paid for it, whereas we have to stand here for nothing.

— They're in those packets with the trademark on them.

— What make are they?

— Lee, I think.

— Lee?

— Uh-huh.

— That's good.

— God, I only hope we can get some though...

— So long as we don't get any more of those stupid jerks turning up.

— May I?

— Thanks...

— We're moving now, brothers, we're moving...

— Well, we've had a bit of a rest...come to the end of our little building...

— Get up, Seryozha.

— They're very practical...you can wear them a whole year and they're still perfectly okay.

— Yes, the material's great.

— They've been learning how to make them over here too, I hear.

— Yes, but ours're still no good.

— Some sort of license they've been given to do it...

— I've seen them—not bad at all.

— Material they use is nasty though...

— Cuckoo...

— Don't be silly.

— Your carnations have almost had it.

— So what?

— No, nothing.

— This is where I was, after you.

— Uh-huh.

— So that's it, then—we won't be getting any today?

— How come? They promised they'd go on till eleven!

— You go and have a look at the size of the queue! We've got at least another four hours to go!

— Come off it, you serious?

— I went up here and there was a woman writing down the numbers.

— On people's hands?

— On their hands and in a notebook. The surnames.

— So?

— They're going to start selling at seven tomorrow. But we won't be in time today... see... there's only two hours left ... less than that...

— Oh, shit...

— She's going down the whole queue so there's no need to worry.

— Have they at least got the line sorted out?

— Yes, it's pretty well spread out, nice and even.

— So what are we going to do—stand here all night?

— No, why bother? You can leave if you want.

— What, for the whole night?

— Till roll call.

— When's roll call?

— At three a.m. and at six...
— What, are they out of their minds? Got to hang around singing cuckoo all night?
— Maybe we could go and come back at three?
— Oh yeah, go where?! I live miles away!
— That's just it, how're we going to make it back in time? All very well to go home and sleep, but there's no transport at three in the morning...
— What idiot thought this one up!
— I think I'm going to leave...
— We've wasted all this time for nothing.
— Shall we stay?
— Might as well.
— I'm going to stay, I live just round the corner...
— Me too.
— Not a specially pleasant prospect, though...
— Never mind, half the others'll give up now.
— Maybe.
— There are lots of benches in the little square up there, we can all go and sit down. This time of year the nights fly by in no time.
— Specially when it's warm.
— Lots of people are leaving, look.
— Good.
— Damn nuisance all the same. If only those others hadn't turned up...
— None of them are going to stay though. Catch them spending the night here!
— You never know.
— They might, it's true.
— Though maybe not...
— God knows...
— Boo!
— Boo to you, silly. Come here.

— Mum, can I have a tomato?

— Not now. Just sit down here.

— Mum, my legs hurt.

— I told you, sit down!

— It's better this way, Lena.

— Quite right, aren't you clever!

— The girl with the flaxen hair.

— The youth with the radish-coloured eyes!

— Little hooligan.

— Hooligan yourself.

— Are they going to start early in the morning then?

— Yes, seven o'clock.

— I think I'll be off.

— Aren't you going to stay?

— Uh-un...

— It's true of course—having to hang around all night. But in the morning we'll be done in no time.

— That's what I'm thinking.

— We could go and sit down for a bit at the station...

— They've got enough people there as it is.

— With lots of benches nearby, what's the problem?!

— You fidgety creature, you...

— You'll be bored on your own though, won't you now?

— They must be about to stop. Time's up.

— I wonder how many they've got left.

— There'll be enough for us, don't worry.

— I hope so...

— There's that woman.

— Is she noting everyone down?

— Uh-huh.

— Volodya! Put it down.

— Oh Mum, just for a bit.

— Put it down, d'you hear me!

— Puss, puss...come here...

— Listen, tell it to get lost, the mangy thing!

— Lenka Penka, little pancake . . .

— If you don't stop fooling I'll poke a hole through you. Bam!

— Ow, that hurt . . . Hey! Lenka! Stop that, it's sharp . . .

— Die, die, despisèd one . . . bam . . . bam . . . bam!

— Lenka! I'll break it if you don't quit!

— Bam . . . bam!

— Give it here . . . there now . . .

— Ouch . . . that hurts! What are you doing! Mama!

— Give it back . . . give it back . . .

— Save me! Mama!

— One thousand two hundred and twenty-six.

— Kropotov.

— One thousand two hundred and twenty-seven . . .

— Sayusheva.

— One thousand two hundred and twenty-eight.

— Pokrevsky.

— One thousand two hundred and twenty . . . nine . . .

— I'm Zimyanin . . . Zimyanin . . .

— Right . . . One thousand two hundred and thirty.

— Borodina.

— Bo-ro-di-na . . .

— What time's roll call?

— The first's at three a.m. and the second's at six.

— Why do they have to make it so awkward?

— Help! . . . Vadim . . . Ouch! Bastard!

— One thousand two hundred and twenty . . . sorry, thirty-one.

— Boldyrev.

— One thousand two hundred and thirty-two.

— Gerasimova.

— One thousand two hundred and thirty-three.

— Nikolaenko.

— One thousand two hundred and thirty-four.

— Gutman. Gutman . . .

— Right. One thousand two hundred and thirty-five.

— That's us.

— Who's us?

— Alekseev... Vadim...

— One thousand two hundred and thirty-six... Have you got a tongue in your head, girl?

— Troshina!

— Just like a pair of kids... One thousand two hundred and thirty-seven...

— Zaborovsky.

— One thousand two hundred and thirty-eight.

— Lokonov.

— One thousand two hundred and thirty-nine.

— Samosudova. What time did you say roll call was?

— At three and at six. One thousand two hundred and thir... forty. Forty.

— Bokanina.

— One thousand two hundred and forty-one.

— Rysko.

— One thousand two hundred and forty-two.

— Konovalenko... Tell me, are there going to be enough for us?

— Yes, yes... One thousand two hundred and forty-three.

— Zotova. He said we'd have the numbers written on our hands.

— Don't want to get your hands all dirty, do you? Just make an effort and remember it.

— But what do we call out at roll call, our numbers or our names?

— We'll call out your numbers, and you'll answer with your names.

— I see...

— One thousand two hundred and forty... forty-four.

— Ivanova.

— One thousand two hundred and forty-five.

— Khokhryakov.

— One thousand two hundred and forty-six.

— Nikitskaya.

— One thousand two hundred and forty-seven.

— Korzhev.

— One thousand two hundred and forty-eight.

— Satunovsky.

— One thousand two hundred and forty-nine.

— Grammatikati.

— What?

— Grammatikati.

— Right. Grammatikati...One thousand two hundred and fifty.

— Monyukova.

— Can you move further back, please...One thousand two hundred and fifty-one.

— Kostylev. Could you write it on my hand, please.

— Afraid you're going to forget?

— Yes...

— Please yourself...One thousand two hundred and fifty-two.

— Barvenkov.

— One thousand two hundred and fifty-three.

— Voronina.

— One thousand two hundred and fifty-four.

— Mine's...Rozhdestvenskaya. Rozhdestvenskaya.

— One thousand two hundred and fifty-five.

— Samosud.

— One thousand two hundred and fifty-six.

— Lavrikova.

— One thousand two hundred and fifty-seven.

— Kondratiev.

— One thousand two hundred and fifty-eight.

— Khokhlova.

— Khokhlova...One thousand two hundred and fifty-nine.

— Chaikovsky.

— One thousand two hundred and sixty.

— Mukhina.

— One thousand two hundred and sixty-one.

— The woman here's just gone off for a moment...she was just in front of me...

— She can come and tell me later...sixty-two.

— Zlotnikov.

— One thousand two hundred and sixty-three.

— Vondarenko.

— Right. What are you doing hiding away down here...

—We're better off here. It's lovely and cool in this little side road.

— So I see.

— Why don't you come over with us, you've got everyone written down now. You can sit for a while here.

— They've...

— Volodya!

— So, we can run off wherever we like now, Lena.

— I don't really feel like going anywhere. I'm done in.

— Tired?

— Uh-huh.

— Oh, come on.

— Honestly.

— Comrades...

— Gets dark so quickly.

— Maybe we should go to the station?

— I'm staying here, Petya.

— So, I'm after you. I'll be back at three.

— Why don't we all spread out in the square, comrades? We can keep our places in the queue there.

— Good idea.

— 'Course it is, there are lots of benches and we'll all be comfortable.

— Come on then...

— Only no need to rush, there's room enough for everyone.

— Let's go, Lena...

— Where are we going now?

— To the square. It's close by, come on.

— You'll have to drag me, I'm dropping.

— Come on, stop fooling around, let's go or they'll grab all the benches.

— Those lime trees are really huge.

— Must be very old...

— There we are.

— No, he's after me.

— Careful, there's some wire sticking out...

— Every bench occupied, look...where are we?

— Over there, quickly!

— I can't...hey...Vadim...

— Come over here...

— It's wet...

— We're here, after you.

— Okay, okay.

— The seat is so hot...feel...

— Great...

— It's been heating up all day...you feel it...

— Toasty...

— It's really nice here, what a treat!

— M'm. You lean on me.

— Ooh, it's just as good as an armchair.

— We're not bothering you, are we?

— No no, please yourselves.

— It's a sweet little square, isn't it?

— Yes, and the benches aren't broken. It's great just to sit down.

— I could stay here forever.

— Put your carnations over here.

— Comrades, are we sitting in the right order?

— I think so...

— We better not get mixed up.

— Don't worry, we're not kids...

— Gets dark so quickly...

— Hey... someone's put on the Beatles... hear it?

— Yeah... where's it coming from...

— That tower block over there.

— Must be.

— *Tiket to raid*... You're right...

— Must be over there—there's a light in the window.

— Yeah... *sheez gonna tiket to raid, sheez gonna tiket to ra-a-aid* ... good recording...

— And people say you can't see the sky in Moscow. Just look at that!

— *Sheez gonna tiket to raaaid, sheez dont ker!*

— It's so lovely here...

— *Now peepl dont ker*... haven't heard that one for years.

— Look, stars.

— You're my little star right here. Little mermaid...

— Don't Vadim. Don't, d'you hear.

— Mermaid...

— Vadim... Vadim, really...

— Young people, you're being a nuisance.

— What?

— You're being a nuisance!

— Look, everyone's dozing off already.

— Tired from standing so long. It'd be great to sleep out here. We've found ourselves a nice little nook. I haven't slept outside for years, have you?

— Me neither.

— Put your head on my shoulder.

— Won't I hurt you?

— Don't be silly. Comfy now?

— M'm...Ooooaaaah...My legs have gone to sleep...

— I've had a bit too much sun as well.

— Let's doze for a bit, shall we? We can go for a stroll later.

— Good idea...Look, everyone's fast asleep.

— Why are you...

— *It vont be long—yeh, yeh, yeh, yeh! I vont be looong...*

— Can we calm down a bit now, boys and girls?!

— That's enough, young man, you can have your sing-song tomorrow...

— Sleep now, d'you hear...

— I am sleeping...

— So warm...

— Feels a bit chilly to me...

— Achoo!

— Oooaaah...oh dear...

— There we are...there...

— Can you move up a bit...

— M'mm...Okay, okay...

— Really got going now...shit...

— Fucking stupid...

— Oooooaaaah . . . ooowaaah . . .

— Achoo! . . . Aaaaa——choo! . . . God . . . aaachooo!!
— Are you cold?
— No-o . . . shit . . .

— Quiet, Petya . . .

— M'mmm . . . mmm . . .
— Oh dear oh dear . . .

— Volodya . . . lie down here . . . put your feet up . . .

— Aaah . . . dear . . .
— Mmmm . . . mmm . . .
— Volodya . . . stop wriggling . . .
— Ghnraaa . . . agh . . .

— Lie still, stop wriggling . . . stop wriggling . . .

VLADIMIR SOROKIN

— Jesus . . .

— Believed him . . . fool . . .
— Okay, go to sleep . . .
— So-o nice . . .

— Mmmmm . . . mmmm . . .

— Ooaaah . . . waaaaah . . . ooaaah . . .

— Put your arm here . . . that's better . . .

— Oooh . . . ooof . . .

— Sleep, sleep . . . Volodya . . .

— Fucking idiots...

— Achooo!

— Killed 'm...'e died...Gaawwd...

— Oooh...
— 'Tsit...mmm...thas right...

— One thousand two hundred and thirty-five! Thirty-five!
— Vadim...Vadim, wake up!

— Thirty-five!

— F'god's sake ... Alekseev, Alekseev!

— What the hell's ... snoring away! One thousand two hundred and thirty-six!

— Troshina.

— Right. Troshina ...

— Oooof ... shit ... shi-i-i-t ...

— It's cold ...

— Aaa-aaagh ...

VLADIMIR SOROKIN

VLADIMIR SOROKIN

VLADIMIR SOROKIN

VLADIMIR SOROKIN

VLADIMIR SOROKIN

— Vadim! Vadim! Vadim!

— Wha... Whas the... why you...

— Vadim! Oh, come on! Wake up!

— What? Whas happened?

— The woman's here. Roll call! C'mon...

— Where?

— There, can't you see?

— A-ah...

— You've been fast asleep... just slept right through...

— Ooaaah... pins and needles... legs like macaroni...

— Come on, Vadim, come on...

— Come on where? She'll come herself... Brrr... it's cold though...

— Everyone else's been up for ages, you're the only one sleeping.

— Am I? Oh yes... aaah... there they are...

— Quickly now, let's go.

— Okay... ooh, leg won't move...

— So I'm supposed to prop you up, am I...

— Okay, Commissar, drag me along...

— Very funny... Let's go now, quickly. I gather half the queue's drifted off.

— Really?

— So I heard.

— That's terrific. Oi...

— You're just like a funny old drunk, you silly...

— I think we're here...
— That's right. After me.
— What's she writing?
— Crossing off the numbers.
— The ones that've left?
— Uh-huh.
— Mum, I want to have a pee...
— You go over there and do it...go on...
— There was no waking you during the night, young man.
— Aaah...yes. I remember. I dozed right off.
— Your girlfriend had to explain. Otherwise she would've crossed you off.
— Why, is she that strict?
— You'd be strict too if you had to go around the whole queue.
— But how—she must've agreed to do it, I suppose?
— Must have.
— So what does she get out of it?
— She'll be served first.
— Great...
— So, comrades...those numbers that don't respond will be crossed off. Certain changes have taken place during the night...lots of people have left...
— But we're still in the same order?
— No...or rather, yes. You've all got the same numbers. But I'm not counting the ones that've left. I'll leave them out... One thousand two hundred and twenty-eight.
— Pokrevsky.
— One thousand two hundred and twenty-nine.
— Borodina.
— One thousand two hundred and thirty. Crossed off...One thousand two hundred and thirty-one.
— Boldyrev.
— One thousand two hundred and thirty-two.
— Gerasimova.

— One thousand two hundred and thirty-three. Not there either? Thirty-three! Crossed out. One thousand two hundred and thirty-four.

— Gutman. I'm here.

— One thousand two hundred and thirty-five.

— Alekseev.

— One thousand two hundred and thirty-six.

— Troshina.

— One thousand two hundred and thirty-seven.

— Zaborovsky.

— One thousand two hundred and thirty-eight.

— Crossed off. One thousand two hundred and thirty-nine.

— Samosudova.

— One thousand two hundred and forty.

— Bokanina.

— One thousand two hundred and forty-one. That comrade's crossed off... forty-two.

— Konovalenko. We're here...

— One thousand two hundred and forty-three.

— Zotova.

— One thousand two hundred and forty-four.

— Ivanova.

— One thousand two hundred and forty-five.

— Khokhryakov.

— One thousand two hundred and forty-six. Missing... One thousand two hundred and forty-seven. Also missing... One thousand two hundred and forty-eight.

— Satunovsky.

— One thousand two hundred and forty-nine.

— Grammatikati.

— Uh-huh... One thousand two hundred and forty... fifty...

— Monyukova.

— One thousand two hundred and fifty-one. Crossed out. Fifty-two.

— Barvenkov.

— One thousand two hundred and fifty-three.

— Voronina.

— One thousand two hundred and fifty-four. Right...One thousand two hundred and fifty-five. Not there either... Fifty-six?

— Lavrikova.

— One thousand two hundred and fifty-seven.

— Kondratiev.

— One thousand two hundred and fifty-eight.

— Khokhlova.

— One thousand two hundred and fifty-nine. Cross out that comrade...Sixty.

— Mukhin.

— Mr. or Mrs.?

— Mrs. Mukhin was here, and now it's Mr. Mukhin...

— Right. One thousand two hundred and sixty-one.

— Sumnina.

— One thousand two hundred and sixty-two.

— Zlotnikov.

— One thousand two hundred and sixty-three.

— Vondarenko.

— One thousand two hundred and sixty-four.

— Sokolova.

— One thousand two hundred and sixty-five. Crossed out. Sixty-six.

— Zvorykina.

— One thousand two hundred and sixty-seven.

— He's gone off just for a moment...he'll be back in a sec...

— Okay. Sixty-eight.

— Vasina.

— Right. Vasina...So, is that everyone?

— Yes.

— Seems so.

— Right. Now for that side road...

— Excuse me, why isn't the queue moving?

— They haven't started selling yet.

— When are they going to start?

— At seven.

— Quite soon then.

— I don't know what you're fretting about—it'll move more quickly now.

— D'you know for certain they've got astrakhan collars?

— I saw with my own eyes.

— Great. The astrakhan ones are so much nicer.

— Of course...

— What make are they?

— Turkish.

— Sure they're not Bulgarian?

— Of course not. Real Turkish. That's why there's such a queue.

— The Turks make them softer. They know the proper way to treat the skin.

— And they're such a nice dark brown...

— Shall we get going, then?

— Okay.

— You're not students by any chance, you two?

— She's a student, I'm not.

— And where are you doing your studies?

— At the Textiles Institute.

— Good for you. You'll be able to make lovely clothes for everyone.

— Not much chance of that.

— Why not? You should believe in your own abilities...

— My abilities have nothing to do with it.

— Now now, you shouldn't say that. At your age we were ready to move mountains.

— And did you move them?

— Excuse me, young man, I wasn't talking to you.

— But I was talking to you.

— Most polite of you.

— What are you getting so upset about?

— I'm not upset. There's no need to be rude.

— Who's being rude?

— You are.

— I am?

— Yes, you.

— Lena, am I being rude?

— Oh, don't you start.

— It was him that started.

— Calm down.

— I'm perfectly calm. He's the one that's foaming at the mouth.

— Okay, you. It's bad enough standing here as it is...

— What've *I* done?

— That's enough, okay? Shoving your ass in it...

— Listen, you men, how about cutting out the swearing?!

— Okay, Mama, my lips are sealed...

— Look at the sweet pigeons, Volodya. D'you see them?

— Can I give them a bit of bread, Mum?

— There...just a bit...there you are. Go on, only don't frighten them.

— I've heard those pigeons spread all sorts of diseases. Epidemics, cholera, goodness knows what...

— That's nonsense.

— No, seriously. I read it in the paper.

— What d'you think, have they started selling yet?

— About time they did. It's ten past already.

— I'm going to buy some cigarettes.

— Does the kiosk open at seven then?

— Should do...

— Can you buy some for me if they have some? Yava or Pegasus, whatever.

— Mum, can I have some more bread!

— No, that's enough now.

— Oh go on! They've pecked it all up, let me have some more, go on!

— Go on then, there you are ...

— We're moving, comrades.

— Thank God for that ...

— Come on, Pasha ...

— Your dress is crumpled at the back.

— Badly?

— No, it's just a bit crushed.

— That's from sitting on the bench.

— We're moving, we're moving.

— That's enough, Volodya. Come here now.

— Oh Mum, wait a minute.

— Come here, do you hear me!

— Look at all those people behind us.

— M'm.

— Queue's still pretty long ...

— Yes ...

— What a crowd ...

— Can we get moving now, folks?

— He's talking to you, Lena.

— I am moving ... you're the one dawdling ...

— They're probably closing up the gaps in the queue.

— The Turkish ones are much better made too. Narrower at the waist. The Bulgarian ones leave you swimming around.

— The Turkish ones have nice buttons. You know, leather ...

— That's right, they're made of leather, I know.

— The sun's been up a long time now.

— Of course ...

— What's it going to be like today, d'you know, hot?

— Just the same, I should think.

— So d'you think we'll make it by nine?

— Should do.

— We're really moving now!

— Yes, it's whizzing along now for some reason.

— That's how it should be under normal conditions.

— If only it was always like this.

— There now, just a bit more, a tiny bit further...

— Don't want to get stuck down the side street like those...

— Not getting too squashed, eh?

— No no, I'm okay.

— All together now, that's the way...what's going on there...

— Great place he's found to turn...

— He'll have to back up...

— You should get into the road and turn around there...

— How'm I supposed to get in the road? What are you yelling about?

— I'm not yelling. You're blocking the whole street.

— You'll just have to put up with it then.

— Hear that? Fucking nerve!

— Wants everyone to stand and wait for him. You turn round!

— Hold on, hold on.

— What a jerk.

— Sends his fumes straight in our faces...ugh...

— Go on then, go on...

— Hurry up, Lena.

— There's no need to rush.

— Volodya! Hurry up now! Where have you got to?

— I'm here, Mum...

— Come here.

— Thank God for that...there, we're out...Ooh, *mamma mia*...what a crowd...

— What's going on?

— This is crazy...But where's the queue?

— What are they crowding around there for?

— Shit...Yet another nice surprise...

— What the hell's...where is everyone?

— This is madness...

— What's going on here, comrade? Why's there such a crowd?

— God knows. Everyone was told to come here.

— Who's everyone?

— The whole queue.

— Fucking hell... and I thought people were buying already...

— Okay, hold on a moment, there's a cop over there...

— He's going to start yapping in a minute...

— Fucking drag...

— You're right, and look at the guy they've brought!

— Let's hear what he's saying...

— Maybe they've run out?

— They can't have. They brought loads in yesterday evening.

—COMRADES. PLEASE BE QUIET. NO NEED TO PUSH.

— Are they really worth...

— Get away from there, it's dirty...

— Excuse me, you've dropped your hankie...

— Thanks.

— NO NEED TO PUSH.

— Come over here, Lena...

— Move up a bit, comrades...

— COMRADES! FOR THE SAKE OF ORDER, WE MUST KEEP THE QUEUE EVEN.

— What's that mean— even?

— So's that why they've all crowded in here?

— Why not cut the crap and let us get on with it!

— What's he fussing about, stupid idiot.

— COMRADES! LET'S GET INTO SINGLE FILE!

— What's he mean, single file? What the hell's he talking about?!

— This is the limit! The queue was perfectly alright before!

— We should make a complaint.

— D'you know if they've started selling yet?

— Looks like it.

— Those Georgians are still around.
— God...this is hopeless. They're going to push in in front of us.
— LET'S GET INTO SINGLE FILE, COMRADES!
— What's the point of that?!
— I suppose at least no one's going to be able to push in like this.
— Oh, come on now...
— Well what shall we do, go back?
— Fucking ridiculous...
— COMRADES! WE'RE SETTING UP CHECKPOINTS SO NO OUTSIDERS CAN BREAK INTO THE QUEUE! EVERYONE WILL HAVE TO PASS THOUGH THE CHECKPOINTS! GET INTO SINGLE FILE ACCORDING TO YOUR NUMBERS!
— Not a bad idea to have checkpoints, mind you...
— Can't see what difference it makes...
— Alright, come on...
— Can you take the bag, Senya.
— SINGLE FILE, SINGLE FILE! NO REASON TO SHOUT AND PUSH! NO NEED TO SHOUT AND PUSH!
— Stupid idiots...
— Oh, stop bitching.
— Can you see if they're selling yet?
— Can't see a damned thing from here...hey, you don't know if they're selling yet, do you?
— God knows...have to go and see...you can't see, can you, young man?
— No.
— Can you?
— No. What's happening there, have they started?
— Should have started long since, in theory. Do you know if they're selling?
— They are, yes.

— You sure?

— Saw them yourself, did you?

— No, that other guy went up. They started bang on seven ...can I get by?

— Yes, yes, of course...

— That's okay then.

— COMRADES! SORT YOURSELVES OUT ACCORDING TO NUMBER! SORT YOURSELVES OUT!

— Are there many serving?

— Two.

— Same as yesterday?

— Yep.

— So now they're going to spend an hour sorting themselves out...can you hurry up there?!

— It's the people in front are holding us up...

— Well, tell them to get a move on!

— You move them yourself if you're in such a hurry...

— Creeping along like tortoises...

— Can we stop moaning, now...been moaning all morning, she has...

— So, back to our familiar street...

— Where's the *kvass* barrel gone? Can't see it anywhere...

— It's further on, in the next yard there.

— Uh-huh...oh yes. Where the sandpit is...

— That's right, there's a sandpit.

— Lena my love...yoo-hoo, I'm here...

— I was looking for you...

— Brilliant camouflage, eh?

— Absolutely brilliant.

— Do you know that joke?

— What joke?

— Vasily Ivanych and Petka are sitting in Headquarters and singing.

— Yeah...

— So Petka says: Vasily Ivanych, the Whites are entering town.

— And what does he say?

— Don't interrupt. So Vasily Ivanych...excuse me...so Vasily Ivanych says—sing, Petka, sing...So again Petka says: the Whites are in town! Sing, Petka, sing...

— Must've been drunk...

— The Whites are in the garden, Vasily Ivanych! So he says: can you see me? No-o, Vasily Ivanych, I can't. And I can't see you, either. Brilliant camouflage, eh?!

— Not very funny.

— There's our barrel, but there's no one there.

— Expect them to start at dawn just for you, do you...

— I wouldn't say no to a drop of *kvass*...

— What next! I suppose you'd like some beer while you're about it.

— No, beer I don't fancy. But I wouldn't mind having a bite to eat. How about going and getting something?

— Where?

— Must be somewhere around here.

— We should get our places first. Be plenty of time when we're back in line.

— You're talking in rhyme now.

— Keep learning as long as you live...

— I am learning, just as Lenin commanded.

— That's right. Keep on learning.

— I do keep learning.

— Learning and learning...

— Learning and learning...they're not getting sorted out over there at all...

— In a moment we'll be back in our very own side street, we can sort ourselves out there.

— The haberdasher's isn't open yet.

— So what?

— Oh, there was just something...

— Oops-a-daisy.

— Why d'you chuck them away?!

— They'd long since wilted.

— All you had to do was put them in water, silly.

— Oh yeah? And where do you see water?

— Well ... you could've found some ...

— Find some first and then start giving advice.

— Don't be cross, Elenka. The carnival's not over ...

— D'you spend your whole time joking?

— That's right. I've one saved up for every occasion.

— What?

— Precisely.

— Ha-ha, very funny ... Hey, what's going on here ... we've gone past the side street ...

— We're going to be in single file now, so the queue'll stretch further back.

— That's a point.

— Let's cross over, we won't be able to get through here ...

— Okay ...

— There's a cafe round the corner here, I know. A proper cafeteria. Maybe we'll be able to grab a bite.

— That'd be nice.

— Excuse me, were we behind you?

— Yes, yes, that's right.

— It's stretched out such a long way now ...

— Move on a bit further, comrades.

— Why, what's going on?

— The queue's getting all snarled up ... move along!

— Let's get back a bit then.

— God, when are they going to stop ...

— Volodya, follow the gentleman.

— So is there a market near here, then?

— Yes, not far away.

— There's the cafeteria. But it looks like it's closed ...

— It's too early still.

— Yes, they probably open at nine.

— Well we won't get to buy the stuff before nine anyway.

— God knows...

— Okay you guys, no need to push!

— We're not pushing.

— So. Have they sorted themselves out over there?

— Seems so.

— You stay here now.

— I am.

— Not too far now, is it? There's a hell of a queue still behind us...

— Yes.

— Listen, I'd just like to go and give my mum a ring.

— Off you go then.

— Look at that woman in her overcoat...

— Must be cold I suppose.

— In this heat.

— Well, it's not all that hot at the moment.

— I feel pretty warm...

— There must be someplace selling *kvass* near the market.

— Don't bank on it...

— Ooooaaah...if only there were some benches...

— Must be some in the yard. Comrades, can you see if there are any benches in the yard there?

— There's a children's playground with some little ones...

— And there are some by the buildings, next to the doorways.

— Maybe we should sit ourselves down there, comrades? What's the point standing here?

— Good idea, why not...

— Just have to bend the queue round there...

— Yes. Let's bend round into the yard now, into the yard!

— Come on then...quick, go and get a place...

— Let's keep in the right order though, keep in the order of the queue!

— We're doing our best!

— All together now, all together...

— It's true, you can really get worn out standing...

— Nice little yard, plenty of trees...

— We're after them, Lyuda.

— It's better over here.

— Give me your hand, Volodya.

— Right by the doorways, comrades!

— Come and sit here...

— Could you move up a bit...

— There's room on this one...

— There, that's better. We would've been standing for ages otherwise.

— This place is taken, he just went off for a minute...

— Over there, look, that bench...

— Good thing the queue's thinned out a bit.

— Vitek, squeeze up a bit.

— Getting a bit crowded, isn't it... shall we move over there?

— Too many people there already...

— Could you move up a bit then...

— Where'm I supposed to move?

— If you'd just shift a bit.

— Move up, Rita.

— This is where the old ladies sit, I'm afraid we've robbed them of their rightful places!

— That's right. We're chock-a-block with the old dears where I live—they're out first thing in the morning and sit there the whole day.

— Sit and stare at everyone, that's right. It's like passing a military guard, going past.

— Well what d'you want them to do? They used to sit on their

VLADIMIR SOROKIN

stoops in the village, so of course they want to do the same
here.
— Lovely lot of trees in this yard.
— Yes, it's quite nice really.
— Look at them, they've really settled in!
— Good idea. Bit dirty though . . .
— There must be yards like this all the way down. The whole
queue could sit down if they wanted.
— Uh-huh.
— So you found your way back alright?
— Just about. This was a good idea . . .
— Take a pew.
— Nice of you to save me a place . . .
— Did you get through?
— Uh-huh.
— Everything alright?
— Yes, fine.
— How are we going to move, though, comrades?
— Maybe we should do it bench by bench?
— How d'you mean?
— Well, all the people on that bench move first, and then it'll
be our turn.
— Fair enough.
— Yes, good idea. No need to trickle off one by one.
— Whole bench should move at once, that's the best way.
— You couldn't give me a light, could you?
— I could . . .
— Thanks.
— Is that today's?
— Yes.
— What's happening in Lebanon?
— Same old thing, it seems. Bombing as usual.
— Barbarians . . .
— They really have a nerve. And those Arabs don't lift a finger.

84

— That's right, they've got used to us doing everything for them.

— That's not the point. The Jews outnumber them.

— Yes, and they've got a better army. America spends millions on them— no expense spared.

— Every month there's some new war going on. Iran and Iraq falling out as well.

— Yes, these are troubled times alright.

— Aaah ... there've always been wars and there always will be.

— But the fucking Jews go straight for the women and children, no damn shame at all ...

— Mind your language, now.

— What's the sports news, anything special?

— Nothing much ...

— Good idea they had—fencing in the garden. It's all trampled on in front of our house.

— Lovely big lilac, isn't it. They must've planted that a while back.

— They just made do with a few bricks round our garden, so of course everyone went and trampled over it.

— But it must have been the residents did all this. You'd never catch the Housing taking trouble like that.

— Yes, I s'pose so ...

— You go to sleep, darling.

— I don't want to sleep ...

— There's a little crossword in here.

— Let's have a go.

— We need a pen ...

— Here ...

— Right. So ... No. 1 Across ... Russian Soviet writer.

— How many letters?

— Hold on ... five. Five letters.

— Sholokhov.

— Sholokhov's a Soviet writer, but this says Russian and Soviet.

— Mayakovsky.

— He's a poet.

— Gorky.

— Gorky fits...

— Shall we put Gorky?

— Uh-huh. Stationary part of horizontal empennage of flying apparatus.

— God knows... maybe aileron...

— Rhythmical ending of a sentence.

— Of a sentence?

— Uh-huh.

— Rhyme...

— Can't be, it's got lots of letters. Popular Italian tenor.

— There are millions of those... what kind of crossword is this...

— Well, name just one of them.

— I don't know.

— Lake in Primorye Territory.

— Does Khanka fit?

— Hold on... yes.

— That must be it! I grew up there... Must be Khanka.

— Segment connecting a point in a circumference with its centre.

— Radius. Must be radius.

— Must be. Heavenly body in the solar system.

— Lots of those... Mars, Jupiter... Venus...

— Five letters.

— Venus.

— What about Pluto?

— Could be Pluto... Move your foot...

— Earth has five letters too.

— Perennial grass in the sedge family.

— Rush.

— Doesn't fit.

— Do you know a grass in the sedge family?

— There are loads of them...

— Capital of the Republic of Niger.

— No idea.

— Hungarian writer.

— Flipping hell...

— Čapek.

— Doesn't fit.

— Čapek isn't Hungarian, he's Czech isn't he?

— Character in the opera *The Barber of Seville*.

— Figaro.

— That looks right. Island on Lake Onega.

— Hard to tell...

— Well, can you think of one?

— God knows... what's next?

— Part of a plough.

— Ploughshare?

— Ploughshare... That must be it. Right, what have we got...

— Let's try this one... Clues down... right. A to Z.

— That's easy, alphabet.

— Alphabet, must be.

— Tributary of the Don.

— Of the Don?

— Of the Don.

— Doesn't anyone know a tributary of the Don?

— North Donets.

— Doesn't fit.

— Tributary of the Don.

— Voronezh, there's a tributary there.

— Doesn't fit either.

— I don't know any others...

— Caucasian wind instrument.

— *Zourna.*

— Right...

— Let's do this one … edible fish …
— In the cod family.
— Salmon?
— Salmon's not in the cod family … five letters.
— The cod family, five letters.
— Trout.
— Trout would fit. But God knows if trout are related to cod.
— Anyway it fits, that's the main thing …
— Science concerning the origin and evolution of man.
— Biology?
— It's got a hell of a lot of letters …
— Can't think offhand …
— Well what's this … process in metallurgical industry.
— Casting.
— No.
— Stamping.
— No, can't be.
— Rolling, maybe?
— Rolling would fit …
— What about this … Kamchatka beaver.
— Ends in 'n.'
— *Kalan.*
— Uh-huh …
— Hungarian writer.
— Gasek?
— He's Czech.
— Hungarian writer …
— How about this … stringed instrument.
— Violin.
— No-o …
— Cello.
— That's more like it …
— How many …
— Excuse me, sir, would you care to stop pushing me?!

— Why, who's pushing you?

— You are!

— I don't think anyone's pushing you.

— Sitting there and poking me with your elbow.

—I'm not poking you with my elbow. We're solving a crossword.

— You might at least say sorry instead of arguing.

— What've I got to say sorry for?

— Oh, nothing! If you've no conscience!

— What about *your* conscience?

— Okay, friend, just hold your tongue now.

— You hold yours.

— Sits there elbowing. Lout!

— Silly bitch, got all worked up about nothing...

— Lout!

— Stupid bitch, fucking...

— We'll call the police.

— Fine, go ahead. Bet they'll come running.

— Young man, you're sitting in a public place!

— So's she.

— Someone makes a slight criticism and you start snarling.

— Takes no notice, the lout!

— What about you, you bitch.

— Stupid idiot...

— Fucking idiot yourself.

— Okay, friend, that's enough of your foul language.

— Why can't she leave me alone?

— If you'd just behave yourself...

— She should behave herself.

— It's jerks like him who go pushing into queues.

— It's you that pushed in, you stinking bitch!

— Stupid idiot!

— For goodness sake, can't you stop swearing! Just like a pair of urchins!

— Mentally retarded...

— That bench is moving.

— Oh yes, they're off already...

— I told you it'd speed up...

— Let's get up, comrades...

— Lena, get a move on.

— You sit with her, I'm not sitting with that cunt...

— Ah look...a flowerbed. That's pretty.

— Could you move up a bit...

— There's no more room.

— Just a bit.

— Okay.

— There, that's more like it...

— Can you read it, Sasha, I can't see without my glasses...

— The whole lot?

— Yes, if you would...

— Right. For sale. Stereo recorder, Mayak 203.

— Uh-huh...

— Pre-fab garage.

— Hm-m...

— New Yugoslav carpet.

— Go on...

— New Viru divan.

— Uh-huh...

— Pioneer revolving stand.

— Right...

— Antique mahogany furniture.

— I see...

— Set of German Language Course records.

— Uh-huh...

— Raduga sound film projector.

— Okay...

— Inexpensive Blüthner German piano.

— Right...

— Japanese stereo recorder, Sanyo 9944.

— Uh-huh...

— Severyanka knitting machine.

— Okay...

— New speakers, 35 AC.

— Uh-huh...

— Arnold grand piano. Inexpensive.

— Uh-huh...

— Tornado mountain skis.

— Uh-huh.

— Mongolian carpet 3 x 4.

— Uh-huh.

— Lomo video recorder.

— Uh-huh.

— Lyre piano.

— Okay.

— Spring-306 tape recorder.

— Alright.

— Child's model railway.

— Hmmm.

— Nikon camera.

— Uh-huh.

— Half a house.

— Not bad.

— Pre-fabricated metal garage.

— Okay.

— Vega 108 electrophone.

— Uh-huh...

— Pictures, antique bronze.

— Uh-huh...

— Phoenix-005 set.

— Okay.

— Madonna twelve-piece dinner set.

— Uh-huh.

— Three-door mahogany wardrobe.

— Ah-ha.

— Stamps, coins, badges . . .

— Okay.

— Inflatable motorboat.

— Okay.

— We should move over now, Grandpa . . .

— Really?

— Look, see, they've gone already.

— Shall we move then, comrades?

— Okay, just a sec . . . but what's going on there? Can we move now, folks?

— Yes.

— Let's go then.

— Come on, Lena.

— You can see now how fast it's moving.

— Yes. If we keep going at this rate . . .

— Hey, weren't those people behind us?

— You weren't behind us, by any chance?

— Yes, yes, my mistake . . .

— Have a seat.

— It's broken, look.

— Never mind, there's room.

— Those are pretty sandals you've got.

— You like them?

— Very much. And what's inside them is even nicer.

— Get along with you . . . They're Finnish.

— They're really very pretty.

— The ones with the silver straps are the fashion now. Know what I mean?

— Uh-huh.

— I'm going to get some soon.

— You've just trodden on an ant.

— Poor thing . . .

— Murderer. Aggressor.

— That's right, I'm an aggressor. And proud of it.
— The poor little ant was just creeping along, and you went and crushed him with your heel.
— I told you, I'm the aggressive type!
— Comrades, I'm afraid I can't stay here any longer.
— Why not?
— I have to go to work, it's after nine already...
— Ah...
— Maybe I could keep my place after you, though, could I?
— By all means.
— I could hop out in the lunchbreak.
— But we're sure to have got ours by lunchtime...
— That's just it, of course...but just in case, I'm after you, okay?
— Okay.
— Comrades, I'm from the other bench. Just wanted to let you know there's a canteen in that building over there.
— On the street?
— Yes. And we decided to go in, keeping the right order, 'cos everyone wants a bite to eat...
— Good idea, why not?
— So that bench is after us, and you're after them, okay?
— Uh-huh. Thanks.
— That's good. Now we won't have to move.
— Look at that guy who's climbed out there...
— Pigeon fancier, must be.
— Why, has he got pigeons up there?
— Uh-huh.
— Look, see.
— There they go, lots of them...
— Uh-huh...
— I used to know how to whistle like that.
— But why don't they fly away? I've never understood that.
— They're tame.
— So they fly round and round in circles...

— I'd fly away right off, Mum.

— Where would you fly to?

— Somewhere.

— Where?

— To the forest, or somewhere else...to Gorky, to Uncle Petya's...

— You wouldn't be able to fly as far as Uncle Petya's. You'd get tired and fall down.

— Well I'd fly to the forest.

— And what would you feed on in the forest?

— Any old thing.

— That's just it! Any old thing! While here in the feeding bowl you've got millet and water. You have a little bite and off you fly, then another little bite and off you fly again...

— That's boring...

— And it wouldn't be boring sitting in the forest with nothing to eat?

— I don't know...

— I gather they don't let people make those special dovecotes any more.

— Why not?

— They spread all sorts of diseases. And people make money on the pigeons.

— Why, do they cost a lot?

— Sometimes. Depends on the breed.

— Come closer.

— Is the canteen crowded, I wonder?

— Shouldn't think so. It's only just opened.

— Probably nothing much to eat there...

— Well, they must have something.

— We'll see.

— It's going better now anyway.

— Uh-huh...

— God, I just hope we make it by twelve...

— We will, we will.

— 'Course we will...

— I'm sure we will...

— Should be there by eleven.

— Not by eleven, I wouldn't think, but we'll be there by twelve.

— Just be another hour or so, hour and a half.

— We'll make it, they're not going to disappear.

— We're moving by benches now—one, two and there we are.

— It's a good idea doing it by benches... you don't move often, but when you do it's a nice clean move.

— What d'you mean, not often. Look how often we're moving now.

— Just hope that lot don't turn up again.

— They won't be back today—I asked.

— Definitely?

— Definitely.

— That's alright then.

— M'm...

— Oooooaaaah... I'm quite worn down by the sun...

— We'll soon be in the shade.

— Uh-huh. There's a bit of shade over there.

— It's not all that hot here...

— Volodya, don't sit on the ground!

— I'm not sitting, I'm squatting.

— I don't want you squatting either.

— They've got a proper garden here.

— Yes, nice little yard, kept it in decent shape.

— Uh-huh.

— Where I live there's nowhere to sit out.

— That's just it. It's either asphalt everywhere or cars.

— Should I go over there...

— No, why, just go behind the fence...

— Alright.

— Isn't he going to stay here either?

— No no, he's coming right back.

— Apparently these ones have a proper lining.

— Quilted?

— Yes, and nice and soft, sort of silky.

— That's good. 'Cos there are some that don't have any lining at all—they're just for show. Much warmer with a lining.

— Of course.

— Even without the linings they're quite warm though.

— Still, it's better to have the lining.

— That's true, you're better off with the lining...

— Do they unfasten?

— That I don't know.

— Should do.

— They probably do.

— They may not, though.

— If they're Yugoslav they should do.

— You reckon?

— Uh-huh.

— That's perfect, then.

— Look, they're moving already.

— Okay then, up we get, Uncle Seryozha...

— Wait a moment, let these people go first.

— Are we off?

— Uh-huh.

— Oop-la...

— Go and save a place, Volodya.

— They don't make yards like this nowadays.

— 'Course, these are pre-war buildings...

— Made them properly in those days.

— 'Course they did. Look at those bricks...

— Nowadays they just bung a few slabs together, completely useless.

— They get them up quickly mind you.

— Quickly and badly.

— They're not much good, it's true. Great big cracks every-where.

— So, just one bench left and it's our turn in the canteen?

— Uh-huh.

— It's on the street, is it?

— That's right.

— Pretty little balconies.

— Yes, the balconies are nice. Nice and wide.

— Must have good high ceilings too.

— Yes, they didn't economise on ceilings in those days either.

— That's right. Whereas now they economise on everything.

— Uh-huh.

— Those days, I remember, come the first of April, everything'd be cheaper—reduction in prices, see.

— Nowadays it's the other way round—things get dearer all the time.

— That's it. Yet everyone complains about Stalin.

— That's all they know how to do in this country—complain.

— And yet he won the war, strengthened the country. And everything was cheaper. Meat was cheap. Vodka—three rou-bles. Even less.

— And there was order then.

— 'Course there was. You'd be brought to court if you were twenty minutes late.

— Fifteen it was, I think.

— Twenty minutes. Once in the Urals, in springtime it was, my late wife ran to work over the mountains, through the ice, so's not to be late for the factory. The bus had broken down, and she set off running. There you have it. Who'd go running to work these days?

— Funny to think of it, really.

— Friend of mine, now, a foreman, was telling me how he went into the cloakroom once, I went in, he says, and there's the whole brigade having a game of dominoes. So he says to

them—off you go to work now! And all they did was swear
at him.

— That's the workers for you. All they can do is get drunk.

— I'd have had the whole brigade put in jail—that'd make other
people sit up and take notice.

— It would, that's right.

— Otherwise they just drink and skive off.

— And steal. All the shop assistants steal.

— You're telling me! They've got the lot, those people, the lot!
While there isn't a thing to be seen in the shops themselves.

— 'Course not. Got their own clientele, haven't they. I'll scratch
your back, you scratch mine.

— And not an ounce of anything for us.

— I went to complain once about one of the shop assistants—
been insolent to me, she had, so I went to see the manager,
and they had their very own queue in there—for smoked
sausage!

— Giving it all to their own staff, that's right.

— That's it. So I say, go on then, give me some. Or I'll have the
lot of you sent to blazes! Raving mad, I was. So what did
they do—went and gave me some!

— What can you do. They're all cowards.

— Gave me two whole sausages, wanted to be extra nice.

— I was at the butcher's once, and I went up and said, give me
three kilos of nice meat, I said, and winked at him.

— Brought it out, did he?

— 'Course he did! So I gave him an extra rouble. What can you
do? The mother-in-law was up from Kirovograd, we had to
have something to feed her.

— That's just it.

— Never used to happen in Stalin's day, though, did it.

— Law and order there was in those days.

— Law and order. And people had a conscience, they really
worked.

— That's right. Exceeded the norms.

— While these days they can't give an ordinary worker the sack: don't have the right.

— The thing is even if they do sack him, who're they going to get to replace him?

— Not a soul to be found, that's it.

— And Brezhnev doesn't give a damn.

— What can Brezhnev do? It's the system.

— Yes...look at that queue.

— I'm just going to run and get a newspaper, Lena.

— Off you go then...Buy me a magazine, will you, *Krokodil* or something.

— Okay.

— Keep away from the driveway, Volodya!

— I'm just having a look, Mum.

— Keep away from there!

— Oh Mum, just for a bit...

— What's so interesting over there?

— Oh Mum, please!

— Come here!

— Is it opening-time yet, Vasya?

— Not yet.

— Let's go and get something, shall we, in a bit?

— Okay.

— Bottle of red or something.

— Okay...My head's all a-buzz.

— There's one not far from here, I know.

— That's perfect.

— Have they got a greengrocers there, d'you know?

— Uh-huh.

— Does it open at nine or ten?

— Probably ten...

— Did you get it? That was quick.

— There and back in a twinkling...

— Thanks a million.

— Ri-ight. Let's see...

— Look, they're leaving, let's go!

— Right, comrades, off we go.

— Is it our turn in the canteen?

— Uh-huh.

— Give me your hand, Volodya!

— Be nice to have a bite to eat, anyway...

— Ooh, my leg's gone to sleep, been sitting still too long.

— Hurry up, let's go...

— God, there's enough people in here too...

— They're all from our queue. There's the woman in red.

— Oh yes. That's okay then, won't be wasting our time.

— That's the start over there, come on.

— I'll get a tray.

— So stuffy in here. If it's like this in the morning...

— There's a menu hanging up there, look.

— Excuse me, can I have a look too?

— Go ahead...

— Right, sour cream, mixed salad... Lena!

— What?

— Will you have the sour cream?

— Yes.

— And the salad?

— Uh-huh.

— And the meat soup?

— No-o...

— There aren't any other hot starters...

— What about the main course?

— Meatballs and macaroni...

— Don't fancy that...

— Fried perch with mashed potatoes.

— I think I'll just have the mash.

— Coffee or stewed fruit?

— Coffee.

— Okay... You on your feet again?

— Long since. Move up closer...

— Ooh, it's wet here...

— Must have spilt something...

— Come and stand over here.

— The rail's really hot, feel it... I wonder why that is?

— God knows...

— Shouldn't take too long here...

— I can't see the sour cream anywhere... maybe there isn't any?

— There is, there is, I saw it.

— Look at that tray!

— What's it got on it?

— Must be paint or something.

— D'you think we'll find a seat?

— Yes, don't worry.

— Excuse me, you two. I'm just going out for a moment.

— No problem.

— Cheep, cheep...

— Stop it, Vadim...

— Cheep, cheep...

— Hooligan.

— Move up, move up...

— Right, let's at least get some bread.

— Excuse me, is there any sour cream?

— It's further up.

— But there is some, is there?

— Yes, there is.

— Excuse me, lady, you've lost your purse.

— Oooh, thanks... look what you made me do! Stand still now!

— Isn't there any noodle soup left?

— No.

— Typical. D'you want some of the meat soup, Petya?

— Okay.

— Could you give me a glass, please, they've run out here.

— The coffee's there on the right.

— I'll have half a glass.

— Have a full one, it's good sour cream.

— Oh alright then . . .

— Let's put them on the one tray, Pasha.

— Put them on mine.

— Can you hurry up there, comrades! No need to all crowd round!

— I'm after you.

— Uh-huh . . .

— What have you got there . . . twenty-six . . . seven . . . thirty-four . . .

— He's got the bread.

— Right. So . . . eighteen . . . ninety-two.

— There you are.

— Thirty-four . . . nine . . . nine . . . sixty.

— We're together.

— One rouble . . . one forty-two.

— Thanks.

— Fifty-eight change.

— Can you move up . . .

— Nine . . . twenty-six . . . right . . . seventy-five.

— I've only got a tenner.

— That's okay . . . nine . . . twenty-five . . .

— You've spilt your coffee, friend . . .

— Damn . . . these trays are so slippery . . . I'll pay for it . . .

— Thirty-nine . . . have you got one kopek?

— Here . . .

— Are you together?

— Yes.

— Thirty-four . . . eighteen . . . bread . . . right . . . and yours . . .

— Thanks.

— Right . . . one rouble change.

— Where do you have the forks?

— Over there ... thirty-four ... ten ... nine ...

— I can give you the change ...

— Uh-huh ... thanks.

— I'm just having coffee, I've got the right money.

— Right. Twenty-six ... nine ... nineteen ... three ...

— You couldn't give me change for the phone, could you?

— I don't have any.

— But you've got lots of change in there.

— I need it. One rouble three.

— Here, I owe you a kopek ...

— Thanks. Right ... forty-nine ...

— Thank you ...

— One kopek change ... can you bring your trays over here!

— Right ... here we go ...

— Are you together?

— Yes, yes ... Lena, come here ...

— Fifty-two ... six ... just mash on its own?

— Yes.

— Ten ... thirty-four ... five slices?

— Yes, five.

— One thirty-two.

— Thank you.

— Sixty-eight.

— There's a table over there, look, Lena ...

— It's taken.

— Come on, there are two places left.

— Can we get past, please?

— Uh-huh. Nina, move aside ...

— Stands right in the way ...

— Okay, Lena, no need to get upset ... you go in front ...

— Can barely squeeze through ...

— Are these places free?

— Yes ...

— Right... put it here...

— You go and get some spoons, I'll take the tray...

— Uh-huh...

— Has the sour cream run out, d'you know?

— No, we got some.

— I'm going to go and get some more.

— That good, is it?

— Not bad. Obviously haven't diluted it yet...

— Here you are, Lenka...

— Thanks. Put the tray here in the meantime, we'll take it back later.

— Shall we start with the sour cream?

— M'm. The man here said it was good, he's gone to get seconds.

— Mmmm... not bad...

— Can you give me some bread...

— Here...

— It really is quite nice.

— You were going to tell me about Hungary, Lena...

— When I eat my lips are sealed.

— Please yourself...

— ...

— ...

— ...

— Mmmm... quite decent...

— You got a bent one...

— I got whatever there was... here, take this one...

— Thanks...

— ....

— Yum yum....

— I can't manage any more...

— Leave it for that guy...

— You're so crude...

— ...

— . . .

— Not bad, the food . . .

— It's edible.

— . . . . look what a fat one I've got . . .

— Lucky you . . .

— Here, take it if you want . . .

— No no, you eat up . . .

— . . . .

— . . . .

— . . mm . . mm . .

— The mash is revolting . . .

— Bad, is it?

— Uh-huh . . . yugh . . . disgusting . . . sort of sweet . . .

— . . . mmm . . . frozen spuds, probably . . .

— . . . It's got big lumps in it . . .

— I told you, leave it for that guy . . . mmm . . .

— Smart ass . . .

— . . .

— . . . . .

— . . .

— . . . mm . . .

— . . . you put that away pretty quickly . . .

— So?

— . . .

— . . . the coffee's stone cold . . .

— Is it?

— . . try it . . . it's just milk . . .

— Yuck . . . skin . . . it *is* cold.

— . . .

— . . . . .

— . . .

— Can you pass us a napkin?

— This is the last one.

— Aren't there any more?

— Uh-uh.

— Let's split it then. Here.

— Thanks, you're a real friend.

— Uh-huh.

— Well, we've stayed the pangs.

— Sort of.

— There's something spilt there. Mind you don't put your arm in it.

— It's alright, I'm watching.

— Well, shall we be off then?

— What's the big hurry? The rest of our bench are still eating.

— Okay, let's sit here for a bit. Though it's not really a place just for sitting.

— So? We'll just stay here for a while.

— Okay... it's pretty stuffy in here though, isn't it?

— It's not that bad.

— Get some napkins from the other table.

— Here...

— So, you got your sour cream?

— As you see.

— Not bad, is it?

— It's the only thing that's edible.

— The mashed potato's disgusting.

— Not just the mash. I couldn't eat my meatball either.

— We were right not to get that.

— Load of stinking fat. God knows what they stuff in those things.

— Are you in the queue too?

— Yes.

— What number are you?

— One thousand one hundred and ninety.

— You're in front of us then.

— Well, we must be somewhere in the five hundreds now.

— Yes, we've moved on quite a lot.

— You haven't been up to have a look, have you?

— No.

— They've brought a new colour, I'm told.

— What colour is it?

— Grey-blue.

— Really?

— Yes, the guy next to me went and had a look.

— What are they like, alright?

— Quite nice. They're made to last, that's the main thing, and they look really elegant.

— Maybe we should get the grey-blue ones?

— Need to have a proper look first.

— Well, obviously...

— You don't know what kind of stitching they've got, do you?

— That I can't say, I'm afraid.

— Be nice if it was red. Or orange.

— By the way, they've got some tea there now.

— Really? Let's get some tea, Vadim, this coffee's disgusting...

— I'll go and get some.

— Go, go and come back crowned with victory!

— Yessir!

— You are a tease, aren't you, young lady.

— Is that good or bad?

— Good. If you'll excuse me making this dumb confession, you're the spitting image of my first girlfriend.

— Honestly...

— No, really... It was years and years ago, but a fact's a fact.

— Do I really look like her?

— Terribly like. I got quite a fright when you came and sat down.

— Don't see what there is to get frightened about.

— No no, just the element of surprise.

— So where is she now?

VLADIMIR SOROKIN

— Haven't a clue. It was in sixty-two, I'd just started at university and got a job on a magazine.
— Are you a journalist then?
— No, worse that that. I'm a writer.
— So where did you do your studies?
— The Literary Institute.
— That must've been interesting.
— Nothing interesting about it...Vile place. Feel sick and sorry just to think of it.
— So what was your girlfriend's name?
— Lena.
— That's funny, my name's Lena too.
— I told you, it's no coincidence...she probably died and was reincarnated in you.
— Come on, don't exaggerate.
— Listen, Lena, why don't you and I run off and find a more pleasant place?
— Where?
— I know a cosy little restaurant. And from there we could go on to the Pushkin Museum. They've got Munch on at the moment. Fantastic painter.
— What about the queue?
— Leave that to me. I can get as many grey-blue ones as I want.
— So why were you queuing then?
— A writer should find out all he can about everything.
— What d'you mean?
— Well, you know...crowds...
— Aaaah...and that's why you were queuing?
— Why else?
— Interesting.
— Your friend managed to fight his way to the tea, I see.
— He's not my friend, we just got acquainted in the queue.
— So much the better, then. I'll be waiting for you at twelve at the entrance to the Pushkin.

— I'm not sure I...

— You shouldn't start out with such reservations, Lenochka.

— No, but straight away to...

— I like doing everything straight away. Here comes your *acquaintance*. I'll be waiting, see you...

— Here's our cuppa then.

— Well done.

— So our sour cream fan's slipped off, has he?

— Uh-huh.

— Funny guy. His beard alone was quite something.

— Yeah...hot...whoooooo....

— Mmmm...ah....

— Slrrrp...

— .....

— Aaah....

— ....

— Slrrp...

— ...tea's not bad.

— Better than the coffee.

— Yeah.

— Aaah...

— ....

— Slrrp...

— .....

— ....

— ...

— ...slrrrp....

— ....

— Look...slrrrp...

— Fool...

— Yeah...slrrrp...slrrrp...

— ...stupid cretin...

— ...slrrrp...slrrrp...oaaah...

— Slrrrp...

— Slrrrp...aaah...
— Slrrp...slrrrp...
— Slrrrp...not bad...
— Slrrrp...
— Won't need to eat for the rest of the day now.
— Slrrrp..slrrrp..aaah...
— Your cheeks are burning.
— Slrrrp...slrrrp...slrrrp...
— Look out you don't burst.
— Thanks a lot...
— Like the tea?
— Mmm.
— Oh dear...what a queue...
— There won't be enough sour cream for everyone.
— Let's get out of here.
— Okay, come on then.
— Excuse me...
— Go through there.
— Bread's all gone.
— Uh-huh...
— So you've made it, have you?
— Yes. What's the food like here, okay?
— Not bad.
— They're going to have roll call at twelve.
— That's definite, is it?
— Uh-huh.
— What, is that woman going to come round again?
— No, we'll have to go up ourselves, and they'll call out the numbers up there.
— That's a better idea...
— I don't know...
— Let's go then.
— Phew...that's better. Air was foul in there.

— Shall we go and sit on a bench?

— Er... I just have to go and make a phone call.

— You've only just called.

— But I have to get hold of a friend of mine.

— Go on then. Have you got two kopeks?

— Uh-huh...

— I'll go and sit down.

— So... see you...

— Tara-ra tara-ra... tara-ram...

— Excuse me, friend, you couldn't help me out, could you?

— What's the problem?

— I'm sixteen kopeks short.

— How come you've wound up a beggar?

— What's it matter... Help us out, will you? Just a few fucking kopeks.

— What're you getting?

— Fire extinguisher— one rouble ninety.

— How can you drink that shit?

— Well, what the fuck... if you've got no money...

— Are you in the queue?

— Yes, I remember you, you were in front of us. That's why I'm asking.

— Have they got vodka there?

— They have.

— Let's get some vodka instead.

— Okay. I've got someone queuing there.

— How much d'you need?

— We wanted to get a couple... didn't have enough cash for four.

— So there are two of you, are there?

— Uh-huh.

— Here then... One fifty... get him to get a bottle. And cheese of some kind.

— Sure.

— It's over there, is it?

— Uh-huh ... Come on, let's go ...

— There's quite a queue there too.

— Yeah, been crowds of people all fucking morning.

— Is he far from the front?

— No.

— Over at *Household Goods*?

— Uh-huh ...

— Looks like a pretty small outfit ...

— Yeah, shitty little place ... Well, I'll go and give him the money.

— Okay, I'll wait here.

— Okay.

— Tari-ra-ra-ra-ram ... ti-ra-ram ...

— Wait ... I can't find ... ah, here's a rouble ...

— Let's go together ...

— Okay ...

— Tari-ra-ra-ram ... ti-ra-ram ...

— They've got some sweet stuff there too—that port wine shit ...

— Tari-ra-ra-ram ... ti-ra-ram.

— And some kind of dry wine ... no sign of any beer ...

— Tari-ra-ra-ram ... ra-ra-ram.

— Excuse me, folks ... come here ... Vasya, this guy's going shares with us. Here.

— What shall I get?

— Get a half-litre.

— You serious?

— Yeah.

— Wow, now you're talking.

— That's the way it goes. I always strike lucky.

— Tari-ra-ra-ram ... ta-ra-ram.

— I'll go and get a couple of packs of cheese.

— Just get one, that should be enough.

— Get a couple, I'll give you some more if that's not enough ... here's some change ...

— Thanks. May be able to get three with that ...

— Tari-ra-ra-ram ...

— Did you find him yourself?

— No, he came up to me.

— Aah ...

— They take empties here too.

— That's right.

— Okay, I'll wait in the street. Can't get through here ...

— I'm almost there ...

— Tari-ra-ra-ram ... ra-ra-ram.

— Do they have any beer here, son, d'you know?

— No.

— And none over the road?

— I don't know.

— There's none there either, they never have any there.

— And they won't be getting any in today, eh?

— God knows. Shouldn't think so, these guys were asking before.

— Tari-ra-ra-ram ...

— What the fuck did you go off for, Seryozha?

— I couldn't wait all day ...

— Fucking hell, I was looking everywhere for you! Come on.

— Tara-ra-ta-ta ...

— Don't push, grandad ... Shoving your ass in ...

— I'm not pushing ...

— Tari-ra-ra-ram ... tari-ra-ra-ram ... when you come ho-o-ome again ...

— Here, take the cheese ...

— *Friendship*. Quite good, these ...

— Mmm.

— Is there a meat section too?

— Yes, but there isn't a fucking thing there. The wife went there this morning, we're in the queue together. Not a damn thing.

— So she wouldn't give you the money, is that it?

— We've only just got enough as it is. She doesn't even know where I've gone...

— I see.

— Anyway, he's just about there...

— He'll soon be through...

— Look at that crowd...completely pissed...

— *In vino veritas*...

— You what?

— Truth is in booze, I said.

— Quite right too...I wanted to get some to keep warm for the night, but the wife wouldn't let me, the bitch...

— Never mind, you'll make up for it now.

— What d'you mean...one bottle between three. Just catch a whiff of it.

— Mr. Universe...

— Ha ha...

— Got any cigarettes?

— Belomor.

— Let's have one.

— Here you are.

— Thanks...ta...

— Tari-ra-ra-ram...tari-ra-ra-ram...when you come ho-o-ome again...

— Can you get out of the thoroughfare, folks. Why d'you have to stand in everyone's way...

— Okay, grandad, piss off...

— Buggers just standing right in the way. Have to force your way through them...

— Tari-ra-ra-ram...tari-ra-ra-ram...ti-ta-ri-ra-ra-ra-raaam...

— Right now, here's the change.

— Give it to him.

— That's okay, you keep it for cigarettes.

— Thanks, mate.

— Where shall we go then?

— How about over there . . .

— What, in the yard?

— Why not?

— Better go in the entrance there.

— Okay, let's go . . . I've got a good deep pocket, let's put it in there . . . .

— Here . . .

— Tari-ra-ra-ram . . . tari-ra-ra-ram . . .

— Watch out, car, Vasya . . .

— I saw . . .

— Ooh, shit . . . been sitting too long on the fucking benches . . . I've got backache . . .

— Shall we go in that yard?

— Come on then . . .

— Well I'm glad we didn't get the rot-gut, anyway. You must be crazy drinking that shit . . .

— We didn't have any money, that's all . . .

— You'd do better to buy a thimbleful of vodka.

— Over there on the right, Vasya . . .

— What about here?

— No, come on, it'll be quieter in there . . .

— Whole yard's been turned upside down. Must be digging something up.

— Doing something with the cable.

— Damaged the tree too.

— Fuck the tree . . .

— In here, look . . .

— In we go . . .

— What are you jumping about for? The big bad wolf'll come and drag you off with your skipping rope.

— No he won't.

— Yes he will...

— Oooh...nice and cool...

— Let's go up one floor.

— Forward march, hands behind yer back.

— Orders taken, your honour...

— Really mucked up the walls in here, haven't they...when d'they last have the place repaired?

— In ancient times when the fucking toads were in charge...

— Put it on the window sill...

— You open it.

— Here, take the cheese.

— Uh-huh.

— Shit...don't make the tops...straight...

— Use your teeth...

— Mmmm...oopla...

— There we are.

— Okay mate, you first.

— Thanks.

— Here.

— Cheers.........phew...aah...

— You next, Vasya, I'll survive.

— ....aah...

— Here's hoping this isn't the last............aah, shit...

— Chuck it in the garbage.

— Shouldn't we give it back?

— Ner...what's the point hanging around there?

— Let's leave it here, someone else can take it back.

— Very considerate, aren't you. Should take someone like you to a winter lodge in the *taiga*, you'd leave supplies for everyone else.

— That's right...

— Slipped down nicely, eh?...

— Not bad.

— Roll call's at twelve, did they say?

— Think so.

— We'll make it.

— 'Course we will, it's just round the corner.

— Aaah...warms your insides, doesn't it...

— Shall we be off, then?

— Okay.

— They're washing the floor there, look.

— I didn't even notice.

— The other day a guy was telling me how this lady went off to the shops and made her husband go and wash the floor...

— 'Stead of doing it herself?

— That's right. So he gets undressed right down to his underpants and bends down to start scrubbing. Well suddenly his balls slip out of his pants and the cat sees them and grabs hold of them...

— Fucking hell!

— Right. So he starts yelling, falls over backwards and hits the radiator.

— Haha...

— His wife comes back and there he is lying in a pool of blood on the floor. So she calls the ambulance and along they come and put him on a stretcher. Well, as they're carrying him along he comes to...

— Shows some spirit...

— Comes to and tells the whole story to the ambulancemen. And they laugh so much they drop him, so then he's completely fucked and breaks his leg!

— Jesus!

— I heard a good one the other day too. This guy was using some kind of solvent to clean something, and afterwards he poured it down the toilet.

— And forgot to flush it?

— You heard the same one?

— Yeah. And then he sits down to have a crap, smokes a cigarette and throws it in there...

— That's it, and he gets blown up!

— He-he-he...

— That's a true story, by the way...

— Maybe...

— You still jumping up and down over there?

— Grasshopper...

— Dragonfly...

— Tari-ra-ra-ram... tari-ra-ra-ram...

— Look at that, mini-skirts back in fashion...

— Legs a bit on the fat side though...

— Bit bandy too.

— True enough.

— Trrrrue, trrrue enoooooough...

— Started getting steamy again.

— They promised there'd be a storm today.

— About time too. It's sizzling.

— Got really hazy, hasn't it. Be a big downpour I bet.

— Should be.

— Well, everyone's pushing in for roll call, what a crowd...

— Where're our lot?

— Must be over there.

— There's that woman, we're after her...

— Where d'you mean?

— Over there, look... over there...

— Right, I must be here.

— Found us at last, have you?

— Only just...

— We're about to move.

— I wonder what number we are now?

— They'll say in a minute.

— You're definite they're varnished, are you?

— I've seen them.

— Good. There seems to be a fashion not to varnish them these days.

— Well, the mat furniture has its own charm.

— All the same...

— Stop wriggling, Volodya.

— It's really steamy.

— Probably a storm brewing.

— That's all we need...

— Lyolya, I'm over here...

— The legs are nice...antique style.

— Yes, so I saw.

— They're so roomy, that's the main thing. Lots of drawers.

— And the handles are elegant.

— Decent handles, that's right. Imitation bronze.

— We've got a sideboard almost the same. Identical almost.

— It'll fit in nicely then.

— Should do, yes.

— Tari-ra-ra-ram...tari-ra-ra-ram...

— Where's your girlfriend got to?

— Can't think. She went off to make a phone call and hasn't come back.

— Maybe she had some things to attend to.

— I s'pose so.

— Might have been a big queue there...

— I don't think so. Aren't many people using the phones around here.

— That's true...

— Ooooaaah...I'm boiling...

— I'm damp all over too.

— Hurry up there, comrades!

— Some kind of jam up there...

— What's going on?

— Why don't they move now, they can have their hen party later...

— That's right! On and on and we never get anywhere...

— Volodya!

— That lady there gave it to me...

— That's nice.

— Leave it now, don't eat it straight away...

— Oh Ira, leave off...

— You've really landed me with the lot, haven't you.

— What d'you mean, the lot?

— The lot. The whole house, and now this.

— Okay, cut it out now. You might shut up here at least...

— Volodya! Come here...

— I'm here, Mum.

— Look at that. Goodness, what a crowd.

— Jesus, what the hell's going on there?!

— Same old thing again.

— Must be the people at the back.

— What'd you mean, the people at the back?! The people at the back are at the back!

— No, it's just they're coming and crowding in here...

— Maybe.

— Not maybe, that's exactly it.

— We should ask the policeman.

— There he is. Maybe he'll say something.

— Where's that woman?

— Can't see.

— Go up closer...

— What a cock-up...

— What's the point queuing at all?!

— Not moving a fiddling inch.

— We are moving... what d'you mean we're not moving...

— We are moving, we are...

— Must be the people from the back.

— Maybe.

— But what are they doing here?

— That's what I can't understand.

— There's the woman.

— Why are you getting into such a panic, comrades? This is a queue and we all have numbers. No one's going to push in front.

— Of course. No need to get worked up. Maybe they're just curious to see what's happening.

— Oh dear, what a crowd...

— Go and sit in the shade, Mum...

— Hurry up, Lida.

— There goes that woman.

— Let's get closer, can't hear from here...

— She's going to climb up... there, that's better...

— Could have stood on a bench.

— Never mind, it's okay like this. Everyone can see now.

— Can you move along, mister...

— You move along yourself.

— Then stand aside a bit... just blocking the way...

— Tari-ra-ra-ram... tari-ra-ra-ram... when you come ho-o-ome again...

— COMRADES! WOULD YOU PLEASE KEEP ORDER!

— There, come to life at last.

— Will we hear her from here?

— Yes, yes, don't worry...

— I wish she'd speak louder.

— NO PUSHING DURING ROLL CALL PLEASE!

— Volodya!

— Comrades, I shall read out... and you... I'll...

— Can you speak up?!

— Can't hear a damned thing...

— Louder please!

— Let's move closer.

— How can we move closer, there are all these people in front...

— COMRADES! NO PUSHING! MOVE BACK PLEASE!

— I'll read the numbers, and you answer by giving your names.

— How many've got theirs already?

— Speak up!

— How many have got through already?

— Right, the next to buy is number... six hundred and seventy-three... that's it... seventy-three...

— Are we only up to there?

— I thought we were almost there...

— That's not that many! Just a bit further...

— Excuse me, they're not running out, are they?

— No, there are plenty of goods. Another vanload's just arrived.

— MOVE AWAY FROM THE BARRIERS PLEASE! MOVE AWAY!

— If anyone fails to answer he'll be crossed out... yes, and the other thing is... the numbers of people that've left already have been taken by new people.

— Quite right. Prevents confusion...

— Maybe you should just read out the names, and we'll answer? Otherwise the whole thing'll go on till dinnertime!

— That's true, good idea!

— Just read out the names!

— God knows, we've stood long enough...

— Just read the names. Anyone who doesn't answer gets crossed off.

— Right...

— It's more logical.

— Hey, Vasya, come here!

— Okay, so names only, right?

— Just read the names!

— The names!

— Okay... So, I won't take the numbers of the people already inside the barriers... they're about to buy anyway... let's start from number... what's your number? You, that woman there!

— Seven hundred and twenty. Kuzmina.

— Right, seven hundred and twenty. So, everyone should simply deduct that number from the number he has already and we'll all know where we are... Miklyaev!

— Yes!

— Korableva!

— Here!

— Vikentiev!

— Yes.

— Zolotarev!

— Yes!

— Burkina!

— Here!

— Kochetova!

— Yes!

— Laskarzhevsky!

— Yes!

— Burmistrova!

— Yes.

— Fedorova!

— Yes.

— Stolbova!

— Yes.

— Smekalina!

— Yes.

— Rybakov! Crossed out... Zvereva!

— Yes!

— Semyonova!

— Yes!

— Sedakov!

— Yes!

— Gluzman!
— Here!
— Chistyakova!
— Yes, here!
— Prikamskaya!
— Yes!
— Razorvaev!
— Here!
— Trupitsyna!
— Yes!
— Karamysheva!
— Yes!
— Kostenko!
— Yes!
— Matveevsky!
— Yes!
— Zaitseva!
— Yes!
— Fain!
— Yes!
— Chabanek!
— Yes!
— Feldman!
— Yes!
— Odessky!
— Yes!
— Bolotova!
— Yes!
— Nikolaev!
— Yes!
— Romko!
— Yes!
— Zhukov!
— Yes!

— Noginsky!

— Yes!

— Brigite! Crossed out ... Yegorov!

— Yes!

— Petrovsky!

— Yes!

— Khabalova!

— Yes!

— Prokhorenko!

— Yes!

— Krivopaltsev!

— Yes!

— Asaulenko!

— Yes!

— Kravchenko!

— Yes!

— Asmolova!

— Yes!

— Kabakova!

— Yes!

— Gorodetskaya!

— Yes!

— Masterkov!

— Yes!

— Davydov!

— Yes!

— Yurkin!

— Yes!

— Sushilina!

— Yes!

— Fedotova!

— Yes!

— Kolondyrevsky!

— Yes!

— Sorokovoy!

— Yes!

— Luzhin!

— Yes!

— Podberezovikova!

— Yes!

— Znamenskaya!

— Yes!

— Titova!

— Yes!

— Popov!

— Yes!

— Krivosheina!

— Yes!

— Zhilin!

— Yes!

— Kuversky!

— Yes!

— Ivanov!

— Yes!

— Samoilov!

— Yes!

— Bendarskaya!

— Yes!

— Kuchina!

— Right... Volobueva!

— Yes!

— Kullam!

— Yes!

— Ilmesov!

— Yes!

— Kokchataev!

— Yes!

— Khayamov!

— Yes!

— Ursunbaliev!

— Yes!

— Abaev!

— Yes!

— Burdyukova!

— Yes!

— Fokina!

— Yes!

— Kalevas!

— Yes!

— Suponeva!

— Yes!

— Nekrasova!

— Yes!

— Skurtul!

— Here . . .

— Khokhryakova!

— Yes!

— Burmistrova!

— Yes!

— Kolbasko!

— Yes!

— Kurganov!

— Yes!

— Kuznetsov!

— Yes!

— Aristakesyan!

— Yes!

— Smolkova!

— Yes!

— Basanets!

— Yes!

— Bolotnikova!

— Here!
— Dzherzhin!
— Yes!
— Batalov!
— Yes!
— Maks!
— Yes!
— Simakova!
— Yes!
— Kazakova!
— Yes!
— Tokmakov!
— Yes!
— Right...just a sec... Marchenko!
— Yes!
— Alekseeva!
— Yes!
— Suponeva!
— Yes!
— Britten!
— Here...she's just gone off for a sec.
— Tolubeeva!
— Yes!
— Spassky!
— Yes!
— Gulak!
— Yes!
— Rubinchik!
— Yes!
— Ponedelnik!
— Yes!
— Petrov!
— Yes!
— Banchenko!

— Yes!

— Gerasimov!

— Yes!

— Yakovleva!

— Yes!

— Nishchaev!

— Yes!

— Pekhshtein!

— Yes!

— Volina!

— Yes!

— Mayakovskaya!

— Yes!

— Tsup!

— Yes!

— Kharlamova!

— Yes!

— Vasiliev!

— Yes!

— Babadzhanova!

— Yes!

— Senin!

— Yes!

— Shikhlarov!

— Yes!

— Megreladze!

— Yes!

— Baskakova!

— Yes!

— Voroshilin!

— Yes!

— Potkov!

— Yes!

— Tarkhanov!

— Yes!

— Nagimbekov!

— Yes!

— Kantariya!

— Yes!

— Kopenkin!

— Yes!

— Pososhkova!

— Yes!

— Baltermants!

— Yes!

— Davilina!

— Yes!

— Plotnikova!

— Yes!

— Vinogradova!

— Yes!

— Samostina!

— Yes!

— Chudarov!

— Yes!

— Shmuts!

— Yes!

— Maiorov!

— Yes!

— Golinskaya!

— Yes!

— Lein! Not there either... Petrov!

— Yes!

— Tsava!

— Yes!

— Chakovsky!

— Yes!

— Popova!

— Yes!

— Baranovsky!

— Yes!

— Zhuravleva!

— Yes!

— Karaseva!

— Yes!

— Vikhreva!

— Yes!

— Lukutkin!

— Yes!

— Sakharova!

— Yes!

— Zhenevsky!

— Yes!

— Kashirina!

— Yes!

— Petukhov!

— Yes!

— Potenko!

— Yes!

— Yashchenko!

— Yes!

— Zamoskvoretsky!

— Yes!

— Krogius!

— Yes!

— Stepanov!

— Yes!

— Siny!

— Yes!

— Srubov!

— Yes!

— Mochalov! Right… so… Kolomiitsev!

VLADIMIR SOROKIN

— Here...
— Babushkina!
— Yes!
— Malinovsky!
— Yes!
— Bokshtein!
— Yes!
— Alpatov!
— Here!
— Nozhkina!
— Yes!
— Semyonov!
— Yes!
— Kruglova!
— Yes!
— Rotenberg!
— Yes!
— Dal!
— Yes!
— Zavodnoy!
— Yes!
— Dvorzhak! No? Cross him out...
— I'm here, I'm here!
— Why not say so then...Ivanov!
— Yes!
— Fidler!
— Yes!
— Kharlampieva!
— Yes!
— Kamzolov!
— Yes!
— Panofsky!
— Yes!
— Dmitriev!

— Yes!

— Kochergina!

— Yes!

— Pavlenko!

— Yes!

— Vipper!

— Yes!

— Melentiev!

— Yes!

— Ikonnikov!

— Yes!

— Galchinsky!... No ... Petrov!

— Yes!

— Giatsintov!

— Yes!

— Klimova!

— Yes!

— Pozdnyakova!

— Yes!

— Petrova!

— Yes!

— Gurvich!

— Yes!

— Lazareva!

— Yes!

— Mikhailova!

— Yes!

— Gachev!

— Yes!

— Orlov!

— Yes!

— Yuvalova!

— Yes!

— Epshtein!

— Yes!
— Narimanov!
— Yes!
— Ryabushin!
— Yes!
— Gropius!
— Yes!
— Kirillova!
— Yes!
— Lebedeva!
— Yes!
— Khokhlova!
— Yes!
— Rozenberg!
— Yes!
— Likhanov!
— Yes!
— Mikhailova!
— Yes!
— Danyushevsky!
— Yes!
— Kurlykova! ... Cross her out ... Viktorova!
— Yes!
— Tange!
— Yes!
— Kerzhentseva!
— Yes!
— Kirichenko!
— Yes!
— Pustovoit!
— Yes!
— Khlebnikova!
— Yes!
— Khazanova!

— Yes!

— Mezhirova!

— Yes!

— Yelistratova!

— Yes!

— Dobronravova!

— Yes!

— Bankin!

— Yes!

— Kazakevich!

— Yes!

— Volkov!

— Yes!

— Krivopaltseva!

— Yes!

— Ryabinina!

— Yes!

— Sotnikova!

— Yes!

— Rabinovich!

— Yes!

— Afinogenov!

— Yes!

— Protkin!

— Yes!

— Kostyleva!

— Yes!

— Nezabudkina!

— Yes!

— Lipai!

— Yes!

— Larkin!

— Yes!

— Dukhnin!

— Yes!
— Nizametdinov!
— Yes!
— Mityuklyaev!
— Yes!
— Volshaninova!
— Yes!
— Shreiber!
— Yes!
— Izmailov!
— Yes!
— Bumazhkina!
— Yes!
— Knut!
— Yes!
— Dobrova!
— Yes!
— Svetonosny!
— Yes!
— Yaroslavtseva!
— Yes!
— Lesyuchevsky!
— Yes!
— Banshchikov!
— Yes!
— Khaldeeva!
— Yes!
— Likhterman!
— Yes!
— Rosenblyum!
— Yes!
— Kashirin!
— Yes!
— Sidorova!

— Yes!

— Talochkin!

— Yes!

— Mironenko!

— Yes!

— Sumashkov!

— Yes!

— Khlyupin!

— Yes!

— Gurinvonich!

— Yes!

— Yagailova!

— Yes!

— Erdman!

— Yes!

— Arbuzova!

— Yes!

— Mravinsky!

— Yes!

— Kolesova!

— Yes!

— Ognev!

— Yes!

— Khmelnoy!

— Yes!

— Zazhogin!

— Yes!

— Dakhis!

— Yes!

— Borisov!

— Yes!

— Narumbekov!

— Yes!

— Khokhmachev!

— Yes!

— Yermolaev!

— Yes!

— Kizyakova!

— Yes!

— Oksanova!

— Yes!

— Pruzhansky!

— Yes!

— Semyonova!

— Yes!

— Vladimirov!

— Yes!

— Gulchenko!

— Yes!

— Poshit!

— Yes!

— Vikentieva!

— Yes!

— Rabin!

— Yes!

— Brainina!

— Yes!

— Nechasova!

— Yes!

— Zabezhin!

— Yes!

— Ivanova!

— Yes!

— Zubova!

— Yes!

— Lukomskaya!

— Yes!

— Zachatiev!

— Yes!

— Lomov!

— Yes!

— Yusupov!

— Yes!

— Ilmetiev!

— Yes!

— Zaliznyak!

— Yes!

— Voronin!

— Yes!

— Geleskul!

— Yes!

— Kholina!

— Yes!

— Vorozheeva!

— Yes!

— Nedopyuskin!

— Yes!

— Molchanova!

— Yes!

— Glikman!

— Yes!

— Tamm!

— Here . . . !

— Vakhromeeva!

— Yes!

— Rebrov!

— Here, here . . .

— Zolotarevsky!

— Yes!

— Grinberg!

— Yes!

— Tolstoy!

— Yes!

— Ashaev!

— Yes!

— Right…Ashaev… Ashaev…Levitina!

— Yes!

— Travnikov!

— Yes!

— Fedakov!

— Yes!

— Comrades, can you move away a bit…Alekseev!

— Yes!

— Monenkov!

— Yes!

— Ryzhkova!

— Yes!

— Sorokina!

— Yes!

— Kosmachev!

— Yes!

— Klyuchina!

— Yes!

— Ester!

— Yes!

— Zvonkova!

— Yes!

— Troshchenko! No… Fazleeva!

— Yes!

— Ryabushinskaya!

— Yes!

— Nemilovich!

— Yes!

— Korzun!

— Yes!

— Vasnetsov!

— Yes!

— Solomin!

— Yes!

— Mityaeva!

— Yes!

— Kotomina!

— Yes!

— Znakhartseva!

— Yes!

— For God's sake, comrades, can you move back! I can't read!

— Move back, what are you pushing for!

— Hey, you, I'm speaking to you!

— You leave off yourself!

— Just keeps standing there!

— It was the people pushing from the back . . .

— Brustman!

— Yes!

— Kharitonov!

— Yes!

— Byalik!

— Yes!

— Nasedkina!

— Yes!

— Rybnikova!

— Yes!

— Litvinov!

— Yes!

— Kazantsev!

— Yes!

— Klopov!

— Yes!

— Zakharova!

— Yes!

— Ravnitsky!

— Yes!

— Slutsky!

— Yes!

— Vorontsova!

— Yes!

— Gorchakova!

— Yes!

— Lyubetkina!

— Yes!

— Novomoskovsky!

— Yes!

— Prishvin!

— Yes!

— Savostin!

— Yes!

— Feldman!

— Yes!

— Korotaev!...Not here...

— Kapustina!

— Yes!

— Startsev!

— Yes!

— Karapetyan!

— Yes!

— Oganesyan!

— Yes!

— Lputyan!

— Yes!

— Petrosyants!

— Yes!

— Bovin!

— Yes!

— Starostina!

— Yes!

— Meged!

— Yes!

— Pozdnyakovich!

— Yes!

— Tsareva!

— Yes!

— Bubnova!

— Yes!

— Banina!

— Yes!

— Nikodimov!

— Yes!

— Oktyabrsky!

— Yes!

— Vsyashkin!

— Yes!

— Zhmud!

— Yes!

— Kropotkina!

— Yes!

— Artamonova!

— Yes!

— Vasina!

— Yes!

— Ivanova!

— Yes!

— Markov!

— Yes!

— Lyublinsky!

— Yes!

— Baturin!

— Yes!

— Karpova!

— Yes!

VLADIMIR SOROKIN

— Volopasova!
— Yes!
— Perlovsky! Cross him out...Sanina!
— Yes!
— Ber...Berbutullin!
— Here!
— Timofeevsky!
— Yes!
— Izrail!
— Yes!
— Kushnir!
— Yes!
— Maksimov!
— Yes!
— Lotinskaya!
— Yes!
— Kuzkina!
— Yes!
— Voloshina!
— Yes!
— Vaseliya!
— Yes!
— Krupenko!
— Yes!
— Dymov!
— Yes!
— Zaitsevsky!
— Yes!
— Bobrin!
— Yes!
— Kuzovleva!
— Yes!
— Nikolaev!
— Yes!

— Marina!

— Yes!

— Kochubinsky!

— Yes!

— Vikentieva!

— Yes!

— Shteinbok!

— Yes!

— Valerius!

— Yes!

— Arbuzova!

— Yes!

— Kiprensky!

— Yes!

— Zamusovich! Crossed out . . . Vlasina!

— Yes!

— Mamedov!

— Yes!

— Kruzenshtern!

— Yes!

— Travchenko!

— Yes!

— Kazakova!

— Yes!

— Blinova!

— Yes!

— Gorskaya!

— Yes!

— Right . . . okay . . . so . . . Bazhenova!

— Yes!

— Tregubsky!

— Yes!

— Starkevich!

— Yes!

— Kanevsky!

— Yes!

— Rokhlina!

— Yes!

— Berberov!

— Berbetov, not Berberov. I'm here.

— Right . . . Savostin!

— Yes!

— Pinkhus!

— Yes!

— Kologrivova!

— Yes!

— Tropanets!

— Yes!

— Dyukova!

— Yes!

— Voskresenskaya!

— Yes!

— Gitovich!

— Yes!

— Kobrina!

— Yes!

— Shapkin!

— Yes!

— Mukhanov!

— Yes!

— Kotko!

— Here!

— Izvekova!

— Yes!

— Shershenevsky!

— Yes!

— Isakova!

— Yes!

— Yablochkina!

— Yes!

— Yusarov!

— Yes!

— Kiri . . . Kiribeev or Kireev!

— Kireev. I'm here.

— Ambartsumyan!

— Yes!

— Makarkenko!

— Yes!

— Tolstikov!

— Yes!

— Ilyashenko! Crossed out . . .

— Dolmatov! Dolmatov, not Ilyashenko. Ilyashenko comes
   next!

— What? Oh yes. Right. Dolmatov. You're here?

— Yes.

— And now Ilyashenko. Or isn't he here?

— No, he's left.

— Right. Kholodny!

— Yes!

— Shnaider!

— Yes!

— Borisova!

— Yes!

— Kostalsky!

— Yes!

— Paltseva!

— Yes!

— Druzhnikova!

— Yes!

— Korablev!

— Yes!

— Ryumina!

— Yes!
— Postysheva!
— Yes!
— Ryabchenko!
— Yes!
— Trusova!
— Not Trusova, Turusova.
— Okay... Kerzhinsky!
— Yes!
— Vozhakova!
— Yes!
— Modelkhaev!
— Yes!
— Vaskina!
— Yes!
— Pak!
— Yes!
— Chanov! Cut out comrade Chanov... Dergabuzov!
— Yes!
— Samostiiny!
— Yes!
— Bugaets!
— Yes!
— Zlobinsky!
— Yes!
— Telpugova!
— Yes!
— Salamatina!
— Yes!
— Zhom!
— Yes!
— Tryapkina!
— Yes!
— Pulyasova!

— Yes!

— Zamaraikina! Not there either? . . . Dyubina!

— Yes!

— Sergeeva!

— Yes!

— Fomin!

— Yes!

— Tyshlenko!

— Yes!

— Sokolsky!

— Yes!

— Izrailov!

— Yes!

— Kerzhachova!

— Yes!

— Nogteva!

— Yes!

— Opanasenko!

— Yes!

— Ivashov!

— Yes!

— Kroltsev!

— Yes!

— Solodovnikov!

— Yes!

— Goldenveizer!

— Yes!

— Trepakova!

— Yes!

— Vosk!

— Not Vosk, Volk!

— Sorry. . . Komarova!

— Yes!

— Vitkyavichus!

— Yes!

— Prygunov!

— Yes!

— Tylovik!

— Yes!

— Kramer!

— Yes!

— Svetlanova!

— Yes!

— Muraviev!

— Yes!

— Voronyanskaya! No ... Dubina!

— Yes!

— Kerzheev! Right ... cross him out ... Los!

— Yes!

— Brondukov!

— Yes!

— Ikanov!

— Yes!

— Zelyony!

— Yes!

— Toporov!

— Yes!

— Sayushenko!

— Yes!

— Medvedkina!

— Yes!

— Boldyreva!

— Yes!

— Klubova!

— Yes!

— Rogacheva!

— Yes!

— Pozdnyak!

— Yes!

— Osetrov!

— Yes!

— Popovich!

— Yes!

— Burlaevsky!

— Yes!

— Kogotkova!

— Yes!

— Shutovskoy!

— Yes!

— Koranova!

— Yes!

— Pechnikov!

— Yes!

— Stretensky!

— Yes!

— Deribasov!

— Yes!

— Barybina!

— Yes!

— Mordatenko!

— Yes!

— Kunitsyna!

— Yes!

— Loktev!

— Yes!

— Voznesensky!

— Yes!

— Barvikhina!

— Yes!

— Zverko!

— Yes!

— Mukomolova!

— Yes!

— Sheinina!

— Yes!

— Libedinsky!

— Yes!

— Knipovich!

— Yes!

— Yelensky!

— Yes!

— Lopatin!

— Yes!

— Fridkina!

— Yes!

— Ivolgina!

— Yes!

— Pazokhina!

— Yes!

— Vechtomova!

— Yes!

— Darol!

— Yes!

— Vanin!

— Yes!

— Lepkin!

— Yes!

— Orekhova!

— Yes!

— Zagladina!

— Yes!

— Trupakov!

— Yes!

— Right . . . Trupakov . . . just a sec . . . Trupakov . . . Volodin!

— Yes!

— Kanevy!

— Yes!

— Dorosh!

— Yes!

— Petrova!

— Yes!

— Lisunevich!

— Yes!

— Khvastunova!

— Yes!

— Izmyzhlavina!

— Yes!

— Valtsevich!

— Yes!

— Novikova!

— Yes!

— Basova!

— Yes!

— Yanelis!

— Yes!

— Kortyzhny!

— Yes!

— Abasova!

— Yes!

— Yurchenkov!

— Yes!

— Menasyan!

— Yes!

— Odalesyan!

— Yes!

— Akhmedov!

— Yes!

— Gazanyan!

— Yes!

— Mtskevonyan!

— Yes!

— Karapetyan!

— Yes!

— Babadzhanova!

— Yes!

— Kobryan!

— Yes!

— Ivanesyan!

— Yes!

— Pizhamin!

— Yes!

— Zhluktova!

— Yes!

— Norovisty!

— Yes!

— Vikrenko!

— Yes!

— Burakovsky!

— Yes!

— Kolomin!

— Yes!

— Korotkova!

— Yes!

— Yarchenko!

— Yes!

— Serdyukova!

— Yes!

— Danilina!

— Yes!

— Makhotkin!

— Yes!

— Dostigaeva!...Crossed off...

— I'm here, I'm here!

— Well why don't you listen then! Just like kids... Averchenko!

— Yes!

— Dobrynin!

— Yes!

— Kamsky!

— Yes!

— Bolshov!

— Yes!

— Khitrov!

— Yes!

— Osokin!

— Yes!

— Korchmareva!

— Yes!

— Drobilin!

— Yes!

— Glushko!

— Yes!

— Pivovarova!

— Yes!

— Vantrusov!

— Yes!

— Kochiev!

— Yes!

— Dubinskaya!

— Yes!

— Shmidt!

— Yes!

— Cherpakov!

— Yes!

— Dolukhanova!

— Yes!

— Kropotov!

— Yes!

— Sayusheva!

— Yes!

— Pokrevsky!

— Yes!

— Zimyanin! No . . . Borodina!

— Yes!

— Sokhnenko!

— Yes!

— Boldyrev!

— Yes!

— Gerasimova!

— Yes!

— Nikolaenko!

— Yes!

— Gutman!

— Yes!

— Alekseev!

— Yes!

— Troshina!

— Here! She's just gone off for a moment . . .

— Zaborovsky!

— Yes!

— Lokonov!

— Yes!

— Hey, friend, you and I were having a drink just now, remember?

— Aaah, yes, yes . . . What's up?

— Has your name been called already?

— Yes, I'm all set.

— You wouldn't like to have a top-up, would you?

— A top-up?

— Uh-huh. I've got three roubles. Maybe get a bottle of vodka
between us?

— Between us? Won't that be a bit stiff?

— Come off it, stiff! Stuff they make now is useless. Bath water.

— Seems the other way round to me—gets stronger and stronger.

— Nah, bullshit. Let's go, eh?

— I don't know...

— But they're going to be yelling here for another hour! And then they'll stop for lunch! Come on, what's the problem!

— Oh, alright then.

— There's a fucking great crowd over there...can't get through...

— Let's go round...

— Okay...

— Excuse me, can we get past?

— You may...

— Fucking cop's standing there fast asleep.

— What's he supposed to do...

— Aren't so many people now, won't take long.

— How about having a bite to eat as well, old man?

— Why, you hungry?

— No, just I don't want to drink on thin air.

— Okay, as you like.

— Let's go over there.

— Jesus, this heat!

— It's boiling alright.

— They're selling watermelons over there, look.

— Over there?

— Yeah, next to the stall.

— Why've they gone right next to the trolley stop...

— Don't give a fuck...

— You could get run over by a trolley...

— No kidding...

— Where's your friend got to, then?

— Vaska? God knows. Wandered off somewhere.

— Watch out...

— Aaah, don't worry. Ought to look where he's going.

— People don't stop much to look these days.

— We'll make 'em.

— Is this it then?

— Yes, look, no queue at all. That's what I thought.

— You're right.

— Give me the dough then.

— Here...

— Maybe you could go and get something to eat?

— Okay.

— Just a snack...

— Alright.

— Right, I'll get in the queue...only five people waiting.

— Fine. Excuse me, is this the dairy section?

— Yes...

— Ri-i-ight...what shall we get...is this the end of the line?

— Yes.

— I'm after you then...I'll just go and pay.

— Sure.

— Right...so...three hundred grams of cheese...

— What kind?

— What do you have?

— Russian, Dutch.

— Russian.

— Ninety. Is that all?

— Have you got any sausage?

— No, there's none in today.

— Then I'll have two bottles of buttermilk.

— We're out of buttermilk. You can have yoghurt.

— Whatever.

— One rouble...forty-six.

— Thanks.

— Fifty-four.

— Ri-i-ight...what have they got there...I'm after you, right?

— Yes.

— So they don't have any sausage?

— No.

— I see.

— Half a kilo of butter and four hundred grams of Russian.

— Excuse me, is the bread section far from here?

— Other side.

— Here...

— Three milks...

— Right...yes please?

— Half a kilo of butter, one milk and half a kilo of Russian.

— Katya! We're out of milk now, okay!

— That's the last of it, is it. Just enough for me.

— That's right...here...

— Three hundred grams of Russian and two packets of milk.

— In a lump or sliced?

— Sliced, please.

— Right...butter...

— Whoops, sorry, I got mixed up. Two yoghurts, I meant.

— You're in a right muddle, aren't you...here.

— Thanks...

— Did you get it?

— Yep.

— I'm all done too.

— We need some bread.

— Okay, let's go and get some...

— Got through quite quickly.

— Yes, no sweat...

— I got some yoghurt instead of milk.

— Fine. Milk's sour anyway, best to get yoghurt...

— What's all this pushing?

— Bombed out, she is. Won't leave us alone...

— Tari-ra-ra-raam-tari-ra-ra-raam......

— Well I'll go and get some bread.

— Get a long loaf.

— Okay...

— I'll wait for you on the bench...

— Excuse me, did you get your yoghurt in there?

— Yes.

— Are they about to close for lunch?

— At one o'clock, I should think.

— They haven't closed yet?

— I don't think so, no.

— Cheep, cheep, cheep...

— Do you feed them regularly?

— Whenever I can...

— So quick, isn't he...look, look at him...

— Cheep, cheep, cheep...

— Fly-y-y away, pigeons, fly-y-y...tari-ra-ra-ra-ra-raam...

— Cheep, cheep, cheep...

— Fly, pi-i-igeons, fly-y-y...

— Here you are.

— That was quick.

— Right, here we go then.

— Look at all those pigeons.

— Ugh...to hell with 'em.

— Let's go over there, there are some benches there.

— Okay.

— Oop-la...can you take one of these?

— They bred all these pigeons for the festival. I heard they let thousands of them out over the stadium, and out of fright or whatever they all started shitting in the air. Right on people's heads.

— What d'you expect...

— Whole fucking cloud of them whirling about over the stadium and crapping everywhere! Crazy!

— You'd think they'd've thought of that...

— And down below everyone singing songs. So afterwards, anyway, they sort of sucked up all these pigeons with ventila-

tors—well, you know, like turbines. They'd bred such an incredible lot of them. The whole lot died and stank the place
out. There were all sorts of epidemics . . .

— Still loads of them about.

— You should've seen them then though . . . so, how about
this one?

— Great.

— There . . . be nice and comfy . . .

— Nice to be in the shade. Here, let me open it.

— Gor . . . fucking . . .

— Won't come?

— Don't worry, it will. It'll have to.

— Damn, haven't got any newspaper . . .

— If you unwrap the cheese you can use the paper from
there . . .

— Okay.

— You go first.

— Okay, I'm off . . . cheers . . . aah . . .

— Have a bite.

— Haah . . . vile stuff . . .

— Don't you want any more?

— Nah, that's plenty. You finish it off . . .

— Be nice if it weren't made of sawdust . . .

— You're telling me.

— Have some yoghurt.

— Mmm . . . . aah . . . . nice and cold . . .

— Aha . . . . nice . . . have some cheese . . . .

— . . . .

— . . . . not bad . . . .

— I was thirsty too . . . .

— Me too . . . . aaah . . . .

— . . . . that's better . . .

— Chuck it over there, look.

— Uh-huh.

— Quite good to wash it down with a bit of yoghurt.

— First time I've tried it.

— Quenches your thirst nicely.

— Good and fresh too.

— Mmm...

— You eat up the cheese.

— Okay...

— Not bad either?

— The cheese?

— M'm.

— This lot's alright. Most of what they make now is shit.

— Yeah. The Russian used to be a lot better.

— Uh-huh.

— Ah, dear... bit of fried lobster now...

— We should leave the bottle for the grannies.

— Okay.

— Right then, my friend. I'll be off. Thanks for the company.

— Okay... you going back to the queue?

— I s'pose so. My wife's waiting for me.

— I'll come too.

— Right then, let's go.

— Cigarette...?

— Ah, thanks... Yava. That's nice...

— Yava are the best, aren't they.

— I'd say so.

— Maybe roll call hasn't finished yet.

— Maybe... shit, look at him.

— He's had a bright idea...

— That's nothing. I was walking along once and this guy was just standing there pissing on the pavement.

— This one at least walked a couple of steps.

— Yeah.

— Look, they're moving... means they must have finished.

— ....mmm....

— Wait, watch out for the car...
— What's wrong with his exhaust?
— Must've filled it with shit...
— Must have...
— Creeping along...completely fucked!
— Things're moving pretty slowly.
— What's the big hurry...
— My folks are over there. Be seeing you.
— See you...
— Excuse me, hasn't Lena come back?
— Lena who?
— You know...she was standing here.
— Standing where?
— In front of you?
— This man is standing in front of me.
— How come? Where was I then?
— I don't know...
— But I was standing here!
— You were not standing here.
— But this is crazy! What number are you?
— One thousand one hundred and sixteen.
— Oh, sorry. I thought I was here.
— It happens, I know...
— But where am I then...
— Somewhere down there, I should think.
— Yes...
— What's he standing there for? Standing there like a gatepost.
— You get out of the way...
— What?
— Nothing.
— Ass...
— Stupid prick...
— Young man, do you mind?!
— What's the problem, can't he move?

— Get completely plastered and don't mind what they say...
— Who's plastered!
— You're plastered!
— Plastered yourself!
— Stupid lout!
— Stupid yourself... what number are you anyway?
— One thousand two hundred and one.
— Aah... getting warmer... must be somewhere here...
— Let me get past, would you...
— Why d'you have to stand right in the way?
— Sorry, sorry...
— Can you get away from here!
— What? Where'm I supposed to go? I'm looking for the queue.
— Just stands there, won't budge an inch.
— What number are you?
— I'm not... God, pissed out of his mind...
— Where d'you manage to get so sozzled?
— Fuck off...
— What d'you mean, fuck off? What's all this swearing?
— Get stuffed!
— I'm gonna get you!
— Ge-e-et lost... jerk...
— I'm gonna... I'm gonna... get...
— Hey, you guys, hey! Come on now!
— Fucking cunt... stupid...
— I'm gonna...
— Hey, break it up now! Seryozha, break them up!
— Stupid cunt... prick...
— Calm down... drunken idiot...
— Stupid bugger... come here you fucking cunt...
— Come on now, come on now, calm down!
— We'll call the police!
— Stupid fucking cunt...

— Get away from here, d'you hear me?

— Stupid cunt...

— Where were you standing?

— Stinking prick...

— Get away from here! Or I'll call the police!

— Fuck off, cunt...

— Listen, superman, get lost will you...

— Look who's talking...fuck...aah, there they are...

— Fancy drinking in this heat...

— H'llo...I'm somewhere here...

— Hello there. How d'you manage to get yourself in this state?

— What's it matter...hic...

— Your girlfriend doesn't seem to have come back.

— Aaaah...t'hell with her...hic...

— Were you at roll call?

— Yeah, 'course...hic...'course I was...

— Why do you have to go and get drunk in this heat?

— I'm not drunk...hic...

— It's very bad for you.

— So tell me...hic...how's it going?

— How's what going?

— You know, how many...hic...be enough will there?

— Enough goods?

— Yeah.

— There'll be enough for everyone.

— That's good...hic...that's good...ooh...

— Watch out...

— Is that our yard?

— No, the next one. The whole queue's in the courtyards now.

— Tha's...why should...hic...

— It's better that way. You don't get so much pushing...

— Mm...

— Come over here now...

— Where...hic...

— Over here now. Come on, stand up straight...

— Ooh...wha's this...hic...

— You go over there in the shade...

— This my bench?

— Look, there's a bench over there.

— But tha's...hic...tha's not my one...

— Go on, don't argue...

— Why sh'd I...si...here...

— Go on, you'll feel better.

— Where?

— Here, see. You sit and have a rest.

— But this isn't a bench...'slot of grass here...hic...

— Never mind. You sit down here.

— Bu'...hic...hic...oh fuck...

— Come on now, sit down.

— Why sh'd I...

— You stretch out and have a rest...

— Yeah bu' why've I gotta fucking...

— It's nice here, you stretch out.

— Oof...oh shit...shi...

— There we are now. You'll feel much better...

— Oh fu...

— See how nice...so, I'll be off now.

— Ooh fu...ooh shi...

— Mister. Hey, mister! . . . mister!

— Fu . . . wha . . . wha's happening . . .

— Mister! Mister!

— Wha . . . wha's this . . . wha . . .

— Mister!

— What d'you want?

— You're . . . can you get up please? 'Cos you're lying . . .

— Wha's this . . . fu . . .

— You're lying on my truck.

— What truck?

— My dump truck.

— Fu-uck...what...fuuu...

— There it is.

— Take your fucking toy then...fuuu...God, what the hell's the time?

— I thought I'd lost it.

— Listen, d'you know what time it is?

— I don't know.

— Where's...ah, there they are...damn, all covered in sand...

— You've got all dirty on your back too, mister.

— Have I...damn...

— I thought I'd lost it.

— What?

— My truck. And you were lying on it.

— Have I still got it on my back?

— Just a bit. Just here.

— Shit...how's it now?

— Still a bit.

— Still there?

— Uh-huh.

— How about now?

— It's okay now.

— Shi...so damned hot...fuck...soaked through...

— Why are they all sitting there, those people sitting on the benches?

— Sitting...aw...shi...fu...

— Uh, mister?

— I'm not dirty here am I?

— Nope. Why are they, huh?

— Sure I'm not dirty?

— No-o. Why are they sitting there?

— Ooof...listen...it's...fuck, I've got some here too...

— Uh, mister?

— Ri-i-ight. Where was I ... fuck ... missed the whole damn thing ...

— Hey, mister, why, huh?

— You leave me alone now ... comrades! What numbers are you?

— One thousand six hundred and forty.

— Fucking hell ...

— Why, have you lost your place?

— No ... just ...

— Was it you that was sleeping here?

— Shit ... where the hell have they gone?

— What d'you mean?

— You know, the other ... the other numbers?

— They've left already.

— What, have they got theirs already?

— I've no idea ... what number were you?

— One thousand two hundred and thirty-five.

— Ooh, well ... must be somewhere up there ahead.

— Up there?

— Uh-huh.

— Thanks ...

— I'll come with you.

— Why, what ... ?

— My wife's up there.

— Aaah ...

— She's one thousand three hundred and fifteen.

— And she hasn't got hers yet?

— Not yet.

— How many to go?

— About three hundred in front of her.

— But there'll be less in front of me, right?

— That's right, must be about two hundred in front of you.

— So I woke up in time.

— Overdid it a bit, did you?

— Yeah, a bit. Some wino went and got me pissed . . .

— Drank a lot, did you?

— Bottle between two, and a bit before that . . .

— S'pose you don't drink too often.

— No, not much . . . God, really stretched out, hasn't it.

— Yes, everyone's sitting in the yards now.

— It wasn't like this before, was it?

— No, that's right.

— But this is how it is now?

— It is.

— I see . . . oops . . .

— Careful. You should give your face a wash. Cold water.

— Ye-e-ah. That's what I need. Been in the sun too long.

— Bad job drinking in this heat.

— Yeaaah.

— Friend of mine had so much to drink once he went and had a haemorrhage.

— Mm . . . over there, are they?

— Yes.

— Wonder where I could get something to drink . . .

— There are soda machines up there.

— Machines?

— Uh-huh.

— Good.

— There you go. Your lot are just a bit further up.

— Oh yes . . .

— Excuse me, lady, is this your handbag?

— No.

— Whose is it?

— Excuse me, what number are you?

— One thousand three hundred and two.

— Thanks.

— Whose bag is it, eh? Just standing there . . .

— Stop running around, you kids!

— How about a game of cards, Seryozha.

— Are they in here?

— In the briefcase, look.

— The yard's further up, is it?

— Yes.

— On the right?

— Yes, on the right after the square ...

— Could you go somewhere else ...

— We're not bothering anyone ...

— God ...

— Vera! Come here!

— Excuse me, mate, you wouldn't have ten kopeks would you?

— Ten kopeks?

— Uh-huh. Help us out, there's a pal. We didn't quite have enough.

— Here ...

— Thanks a lot ... What's up, you hungover?

— A bit.

— Come along with us, then. Hair of the dog.

— No, I can't ...

— Here, Petya, off you go ...

— Excuse me, what number are you?

— One thousand two hundred and seventy-five.

— Thanks ... aaah, there they are ...

— Volodya! Leave the boy alone!

— So I've found you at last ...

— Ah ... hello there. How've you got yourself so dirty?

— Dirty?

— Been drinking, I suppose?

— Well, just a bit ... so, what's happening? Will we soon be there?

— Shouldn't be long now.

— How many still in front?

— About two hundred and fifty. No more than that.

— Great...

— You've got yourself a bit grubby here...

— Ah, thanks...goodness, yes...

— Your girlfriend never turned up.

— Didn't she?

— No-o.

— Something must've cropped up I suppose...probably had to attend to something...

— Have a seat...could you make room for our friend here? He was in the queue.

— Thanks.

— The whole queue's moving from yard to yard now. The police asked us to wait in the courtyards so's not to block the street.

— I see...

— We've only got about two more to go now...

— Service quite quick now, is it?

— Yes, there are four of them serving.

— Four? That's great.

— Yes...

— Excuse me, young man, if I might ask, I'd be more comfortable if...

— Yes, yes, of course...

— Ah, that's better...thanks...you've got a bit of sand on you, you know...

— Ah...yes...

— Whew...well, it's clouded over anyway.

— Be raining soon.

— They promised a storm.

— Why don't you come and stand here?

— Thanks.

— Volodya!

— Like a sandwich, Lyusya?

— Oh, thanks.

— It's always the way. Look after number one and don't give a damn about us.

— That's right...

— And this lot can't stop chasing that ball. All day long they've been at it. All they can think of is football...

— His name's Vorontsov... Vorontsov...

— Thanks... ta.

— It's just wicked, really... downright disgraceful.

— I think she'll be here in a minute...

— We'll see...

— Volodya! Will you listen to me!

— Feel free, help yourself.

— There wasn't any roll call while I was away was there?

— No.

— Good...

— Though quite a lot of people have left and given their names to someone else.

— I see...

— And there've been speculators turning up.

— They turn up everywhere...

— Apparently the price of a name in the first hundred is fifteen roubles.

— Not bad... God... my head's splitting...

— Been in the sun too long?

— M'm, a bit...

— We used to be worse off, of course, no doubt about it, but people were more decent in those days... there were plenty of good folks around. But nowadays it's every man for himself...

— I'm Svetlana Yakovlevna.

— It's a pleasure. Igor Ivanovich.

— Nice to meet you.

— Volodya!

— I just hope those great louts don't knock him . . . look, look at them, running around like madmen . . .

— How often do we move?

— Well, we're moving yard by yard now.

— Good idea. It was stupid just bench by bench . . . better for the whole yard to move.

— Yes, it's better that way . . .

— Stupid pricks . . .

— I'd saved a place behind him, and when I come back he says I wasn't there—you weren't here, he says! I ask you!

— How stupid can you get.

— It's not just stupid, it's downright criminal . . .

— Throw the crumbs in there . . . and the paper . . .

— Heavy going, though.

— This yard isn't too bad, really. The benches in the other one were broken . . .

— Not over there, Seryozha.

— I wasn't . . .

— Not much further to go now . . .

— I was beginning to worry they'd all be sold.

— Don't worry, there'll be plenty for us.

— There's plenty, plenty . . .

— I spent some time there working myself, mind . . .

— Well, it's not such a bad place.

— Of course. Still, pretty dull though.

— Volodya! What's all this rubbish!

— I saw a funny scene at the supermarket the other day.

— What was that?

— There was this gigantic queue, but the shelves were completely bare.

— Completely?

— That's right. But behind the glass doors at the back you could see the shop people packing up these sausages. Whole mountain of them.

— Uh-huh.

— And then they put the whole heap on the shelves.

— And?

— It was like one huge piranha fish! Before you could count to three, the whole lot had gone. And there were the shelves completely bare again, but the way the crowd looked then! —so pleased with themselves, just waiting there to pay...

— I once saw two women fighting with sausages.

— Handy weapons... haha...

— The liverwurst type— two ninety a kilo...

— Ha, ha, ha!

— Move up, let him sit down...

— You wouldn't have a cigarette, would you?

— Uh-huh... here...

— Thanks...

— It's knitted, you see.

— Aaaaah... that's nice...

— They've got tomatoes there. You never get them here.

— Rostov. Quite a good make. It's got a through channel.

— What's that?

— It means when you're taping something you can hear how it's coming out.

— Nice.

— Mendelssohn.

— I thought it was Weber.

— No, *Songs without Words*.

— Can you chuck us some bread, Senya...

— Here...

— There, that's better.

— Ooh, a wasp... get it away...

— Don't worry, it won't sting you . . .

— That's what they themselves want, d'you see?! That's what they want!

— Can you move along, move along please . . .

— That's nothing compared to the size you sometimes get . . .

— There he goes.

— Can you give me a bit. I just want to try it.

— Not exactly hurrying, is he . . . what a weirdo.

— Sharpe are not bad either. Thirty watts. Cost three hundred roubles, if not more . . .

— GVC's thirty watts too. You've got your tuner and the whole lot in one . . .

— That's an old joke.

— Volodya!

— I'm not buying them for myself anyhow. My son asked me. He's in the army.

— He's the dregs, really.

— Oh yeah, I bet they'll write about it . . .

— Maybe they will, you never know. Now that they're cracking down on the speculators.

— Aah, they don't give a damn.

— What the fuck . . . ?

— Anyway, big deal . . .

— Fucking hell, it was just standing there, wasn't in anyone's way . . .

— Valya, Valya . . .

— Married someone much older . . .

— Didn't she want a young one then?

— Ah, she'd got her head screwed on alright.

— They've all become such cunning little bitches . . . don't marry for love like in the old days.

— Ah, who's talking about love! They've got their own ideas these days . . .

— Load of crap . . .

— Blokhin in Dynamo kept looking back at mid-field, he wasn't exactly pleased, felt everything was going wrong...

— 'Course, you've got to know how to play...

— What I can't get over is why out of two hundred and fifty million people they can't pick twelve that are capable of kicking a ball around!

— Ah, to hell with them! There aren't even any real coaches left either. They're all just careerists.

— That's right...

— Sickening to watch...

— And Ozerov, stupid asshole, kept blathering on and on over the mike...Our fellows! Our fellows!

— Everything depends on the speakers.

— He's such a jerk.

— Awful...it's incredible...

— No. Scriabin and Rakhmaninov graduated together. Only Rakhmaninov got a big gold medal, and Scriabin a little one.

— No, that's not fair.

— Basov's cassettes are better. Much finer...

— Shit...

— Viktor Nikolaich! Come over here with us!

— Can't bear listening to him. He's got such a stammer...

— Tari-ra-tara-raam.

— He's just got back from America.

— And how was it?

— Depends...There's an awful lot of crime. You can't really go out after eight in the evening...There's loads of stuff around to buy, but you have to work like a horse.

— Of course. Can't get anything for nothing.

— Here at least you can walk round the streets at night.

— I wouldn't speak too soon. Just in the last two years we've had two murders round our house. And robbery.

— Just coincidence.

— Oh yeah, you reckon!

— The point is Americans are always scared about something—frightened they'll be kicked out of their job or their wife's going to get raped or their car stolen . . . they're scared stiff the whole time . . .

— Still, they don't have these queues.

— No, they don't have the queues, that's true . . .

— They have to work their asses off over there, but here if you come drunk to work it's no big deal.

— That's right . . .

— Obviously the Beatles were great, but they've had their day. There are some interesting new groups now. Police and Led Zeppelin. The Stones still produce good things from time to time.

— They're okay.

— But the cars are fantastic. Cars, roads, technology . . .

— Of course . . .

— He just drank and drank and got so fucking pissed he fell straight down from the fifth floor.

— Ha ha ha . . .

— Sickening really.

— Tari-ra-ra-raam . . .

— Double album. But after their concert album they just fell apart . . .

— 'Course, they make a great thing of their freedom over there. You can yell about Reagan being an idiot, that's a fact, but when it comes to saying your boss is an idiot, that's another matter—you'll get the sack.

— Uh-huh . . .

— Prick was a fucking kilometre long. She took one look at it and squealed like a rat . . .

— I prefer the Stones myself.

— There's always the cooking to fit in, and then this, that and the other . . .

— Right in there, spot on.

— A friend of mine was saying the same thing, soon as I stick mine in a woman, he says, she bursts into tears. God knows why...

— Good thing I woke up in time.

— Shit.

— Wipe up after you... you've spilt something...

— God knows. A boss is a boss...

— Come here.

— Right next to Yashin, no less.

— Come off it...

— Honestly!

— Ah, come on...

— Saleswoman shouts to the whole shop—whose check is this, comrades? And he just keeps his mouth shut, the bastard.

— Should get one in the mug for things like that.

— I'd have the lot of them shot if you asked me.

— There's no roach to be had anywhere.

— Life is fine there for people who've got money. But the poor, like they were showing us on *Vremya*—they're left to sleep on the pavement.

— Well, that's what they show us here. If you believe them...

— Still a virgin, she was. Cried, didn't want to do it. Had to talk her into it...

— Ha ha...

— Fucking awful record. Graffiti are better...

— They shrink in the wash.

— Badly?

— No, not too bad...

— No, there wasn't much blood. But it hurt when I got it up her the second time...

— There was a queue for them in GUM...

— A long one?

— Not really. My friend managed to get some.

— You can never tell where they're going to bring them out...
— No-o, that's right...
— Rouble forty-three...
— That all?!
— Yes.
— I heard they started firing at the Zeppelins at that concert.
— It was just water. They were all okay.
— I heard their drummer was killed...
— I didn't hear about that.
— She was a sweet little girl, too...
— Bit of alright, was she?
— Little red-head, real softie. Armpits smelt lovely...
— I drew up a fifth one, but when I went to consult him he wouldn't take it.
— Why?
— Ah, he said, on supports like that the thing won't hold up at all.
— Fucking idiot...
— Anyway, when I stuffed my calculations straight in his face, he just laughed.
— They're all jerks in that department.
— So in the morning I was packing my suitcase, and there she was in tears. I can't live without you, she says.
— What did you do?
— I calmed her down, gave her some money. Promised I'd come straight back as soon as I got another business trip...
— And did you ever go back?
— Why should I go back there? No one in his right mind would go to a dump like that more than once. Back of beyond it was...
— I like the Hippies' fifth. They really let themselves go...
— They're great on the keyboard.
— Keyboard and vocal are both pretty good.
— Who's their lead guitar?

— Box.

— And who's on the keyboard—Hensley?

— Hensley...

— You wait and wait, and what's it all for?

— That quick!

— Uh-huh...

— I haven't had a good fuck for ages either.

— Having a child so late, of course...difficult business.

— He's had things in *Yunost*, I think. And then a book of his came out.

— Interesting?

— Yeah, not bad. Detective story.

— Have you read *A Shot in the Back*?

— No.

— That's quite good too. Murder mystery. The friend kills him.

— Look, everyone's going to start running now.

— Are we going to move soon, d'you know?

— I don't know. They should say.

— They'll tell us.

— To hell with Trusov, the stupid shit. You can't frighten me with that.

— Volunteer...

— Uh-huh.

— Handles are imitation bronze. It's sort of glazed.

— Completely fucked out.

— Listen, can you stop leaning on everyone?!

— Who's leaning on everyone?

— Aren't you?

— Who's leaning on everyone?

— You're the one leaning. Move up!

— By all means.

— Pushes right up close and just sits there...

— Looks like him.

— 'Course, as you know, it's difficult to force ones like that...

— I know...

— Ooaaaah...phew...

— Tari-ra-ra-raam...

— Come on, let's have a game. Your throw!

— No, I don't feel like it.

— Tired, are you?

— No, I'm not tired, I just don't feel like it.

— What's the matter, such a little kid and you don't want to play?

— I don't want to.

— I'd like to have a crap, but...

— Why don't you go behind those containers?

— You don't have any paper, do you?

— Take the newspaper.

— They're not up to much either.

— Yeah?

— Yeah. Still, while the going's good...

— Well, the Beatles are classics, obviously.

— Through Sergei Anatolich...

— Did he agree?

— Well, he didn't do it for nothing, of course.

— But they did it, did they?

— Uh-huh.

— And how is it?

— Perfectly alright, stands up okay.

— I'm hunting for one like that too.

— You can get them in *World*.

— He's a good guy, he was in my class.

— Nice to fly down there in the autumn—loads of fruit and vegetables...

— To hell with the brown ones! I want grey.

— I don't really care what colour I get.

— Tari-ra-ra-raam...

— Maybe we're going to move on now...

— Just one more to go and that's it?

— No, it's a bit further after that.

— Excuse me, do you remember, was there a woman queuing here?

— In red?

— Yes.

— She's gone off somewhere...

— She's gone?

— Uh-huh...

— Why d'you have to go on and on... You can't do this, can't do that!

— Well, fuck it... you really shouldn't...

— Why not! Everything's allowed here!

— They're not going to sell it to you, that's all...

— If I give them a tenner each they will...

— What if they don't...

— Ah, come off it, they're not going to refuse.

— Tanya, go and give Mum a ring.

— Will you stay here?

— Yes.

— The sun's clouded over... look at that big cloud, Mum...

— There's going to be a storm...

— Yes... it clouded over so quickly...

— There's that woman.

— Are we moving?

— I think so...

— Comrades, we're moving on to the next yard!

— At long last...

— Get up, Vasya...

— Come here, Volodya! We're moving.

— I told you it'd go quickly now...

— Get up, lads.

— It's over there, take it.

— Oh, shit, my legs have gone to sleep.

— Off we go...

— No need to hurry...where are you rushing off to?!

— Complete havoc they've made here.

— All these yards are in a total mess. They're laying a cable...

— You can get through here.

— Ah yes...

— Can you help me, Seryozha...

— Give me your hand...

— Over there, look...where are you...

— Those benches?

— Don't push, friends! What are you shoving for?!

— We're not shoving...

— You're shoving yourself, stupid ass...

— Sit down in the right order.

— I'm here, Sasha!

— There's thunder on the way...

— God, it's gone so dark...

— We're going to get soaked now...

— There's been no rain for a week...

— Maybe it'll blow over?

— Not likely! It's got so dark...and cool...

— Yes. There's going to be a thunderstorm.

— There is.

— Stupid wanker carried on for a while and I just left...

— It's completely clouded over...Come on, let's get into the doorways...Vitya...

— Ooh...let's go...

— Sashka! Let's go...

— Come on, hurry up...

— Oh, shit... fuck...

— Let's run for it!

— Volodya! Come here! Come here you silly!

— Just like that! Let's run!

— Hey...Zhenya...Zhenya...

— Come over here! Where are you going?!
— It's too far!
— Bitch...
— Come here, Viktor Petrovich!
— Oh God, holy mother...
— Go on, Vasya, take to your heels...
— Fuck, we'd hardly sat down...
— That one's nearer, that one!
— Uh-huh...
— The-ere.
— Get right in there!
— Hurry up, hurry up!
— Fucked in the gob he was...cunt...
— Sasha, hold on...
— Nor frost nor heat we fear...
— That's more like it.
— Did you get very wet?
— No...not too bad...
— Came down so quickly, didn't it?
— Look! Look! Look at that!
— Wow! What a downpour...
— Look at it, look—it's absolutely white!
— Ooh...this is going to go on some time...
— Look at it, look!
— M'm...
— Am I very wet?
— Really, young man, how've you...
— Phew...ooh...I only just made it...phew...
— How come you took so long?
— Ooooh...pretty wet, aren't I?
— Soaked to the skin...
— Phew...sure is raining...phew...
— Really bucketing down, straight out of the barrel...
— Phew...ooh...

— Why don't you go up to the next floor and wring your shirt
out up there.

— Phew…that's what I'll have to do…ooh…

— It's like in the jungle.

— Yeah…

— Would you like some help?

— No no, it's alright…phew…thanks…

— Rain, rain, rain…

— Phew…oh, shit…what, up there?

— If you go straight upstairs…

— Uh-huh…wow, it's dark…shit…

— Ooh!

— Whoops!…I'm so sorry…

— Ooh, you gave me such a fright…what a nightmare!

— Sorry…I'm completely drenched…sorry…

— Goodness. You're shining all over…where did you get so
soaked?

— Right here. I'm in the queue…that's how I fetched up
here.

— Aaaah. I see. Well, you've certainly had a soaking…

— Are you in the queue too?

— No, I live here.

— Aah…

— I just came out to have a smoke. And found a water-sprite at
my door!

— Is that what I look like?

— Exactly.

— Ye-es…you couldn't give me a cigarette, could you?

— Yes, come on in.

— But I'm all wet…I'd better stay out here…

— No no, come on, you can't stand there shivering on the
stairs.

— Thanks…

— Hold on, I'll just get the mail…ah…oh well, maybe next

time. Right, come along then.

— Nice lining you've put on the door...

— D'you like it?

— Yes, very elegant...

— Come in.

— How can I come in in this state...

— Don't worry, there's no one here.

— Do you live on your own?

— I guess so...

— You could get lost here all by yourself...who could've deserted a beauty like you?

— Ah, someone, someone...here...

— Thanks. Have you got a light...

— Here...

— Thanks...mmm...thank you...

— Do come in.

— No no, I really couldn't.

— Come on, you can't stand there in the corridor.

— But I'm soaking wet...

— I tell you what, if you go into the bathroom and take off your shirt I'll dry it out with the iron.

— No, I couldn't possibly...putting you to all this bother...

— Go on, take it off.

— No, I'm embarrassed...

— Take it off before I change my mind.

— Really, I'm embarrassed...

— Take it off quickly, I'll give you a dressing gown in the meantime.

— Such a mess...damn...it's all stuck to me...

— How come you didn't make it in time?

— Oh, I'd sort of nodded off sitting on a bench, just snoozing a bit...or rather I was planning to have a little nap...and then...God, it's all sticking to me...

— Down came the rain, eh?

— Uh-huh. Not just rain—it was like a deluge in South America.

— Haha...

— The heavens just opened...there...I've taken it off...

— Here's the dressing gown.

— Thanks...I still don't know my saviour's name...

— Lyudmila Konstantinovna. You can call me Lyuda.

— And I'm Vadim.

— Uh-huh...it's soaked...come in here...

— It's so long...where's it from, Japanese?

— The dressing-gown? No, I made it myself.

— You must be a terrific seamstress.

— Ah, simple little job...what did I do with the iron...

— Cosy place you've got here...nice to have it so shady...

— It's because of what they're putting up in the street, that's why it's so shady.

— No, but generally...who did these paintings?

— The same someone. The hand that killed the deer.

— Ah...your husband?

— Ex...

— Interesting work. I like this landscape...

— Oh, it's all derivative stuff...

— No, why d'you say that?

— I don't know. I don't understand a thing about it, but that's how it looks to me.

— And what do you do for a living?

— Economist.

— How interesting...

— It's not interesting at all. Very dull in fact.

— Well, of course, it depends where you work...

— Aaah...makes no difference...

— D'you mind if I smoke here, Lyudmila Konstantinovna?

— No no, by all means, smoke to your heart's content...

— And my body's destruction.

— Whatever...

— Nice high ceilings you've got.

— Yes. That's the one advantage of the place...

— Why the one advantage? You've got a nice big room. They don't make one-room places like this any more.

— There... we'll just let it warm and I'll iron your shirt for you...

— I don't know what I would have done without you...

— I suppose everyone in the queue ran into the doorways?

— Yes, we all ran in like a bunch of mice...

— When I went out to the shops earlier on I had a look at the queue. If you don't mind me saying so, it's pretty crazy having everyone in the courtyards.

— Yes, well, of course...

— Everyone sitting on the benches like a bunch of paralytics! No room for anyone to come out and sit down. You should queue out there on the street...

— Yes... what can I say... it's the police who masterminded the whole thing...

— Idiots...

— I've been cursing that I got involved in the first place. It's a real epic, this queue...

— Been there long?

— Not all that long...

— It's absolutely gigantic. I haven't seen a queue like that in a long time.

— Well, it's once in a blue moon they give us stuff like that.

— Yes. Everyone nowadays wants to live in style...

— That's right...

— You've got a bit of dirt on it here... bit of sand or something...

— Aaah... I was playing volleyball with some friends and I fell over...

— Sportsman, are you?

— No, not really.

— And what do you do for a living?

— Work for a little journal.

— Which one?

— Oh, just a technical journal...

— You're a journalist then.

— I used to want to be...no, I'm an editor.

— Where did you do your studies?

— Three different places. Didn't graduate from any of them.

— Which ones?

— Moscow University, Teacher's Training and the Steel and Alloys Institute.

— That's quite a mixture...did you study for long?

— Depends. I was a year at the University, three at the Teacher's Training and two at the other.

— And you didn't graduate from any of them?

— No.

— What got in the way?

— Oh, everything, everything got in the way.

— What d'you mean, everything?

— Well, what with one thing and another...I was studying history, and I got more interested in technical things. And then at the Steel and Alloys it was the other way round— started me thinking about history again.

— That's interesting...

— Fascinating...is this an ashtray?

— Yes.

— Funny little piece.

— There—your shirt's ready...here, take it...

— I can't thank you enough, Lyudmila Konstantinovna.

— You're welcome...

— Ooh, it's got even darker. What's going on there...

— Well, there hasn't been rain for so long. The sky's simply burst...

— That's right.

— So tell me, Vadim, what made you decide to get in a queue like this?

— That's a strange question.

— No no, I understand, but it seems a bit strange for a man to spend his summer queuing up...

— Well, I wasn't really queuing for myself but for a friend. He really wanted me to, so when the chance arose...

— You're a real friend, aren't you...

— I don't know. Anyway, the thing is I'm on holiday, I haven't got to rush off anywhere. I'm not planning to go away...

— Why not?

— Oh, I've got sick of the scrum down South. I've been going to the South for the last ten years. Either there or the Baltic...

— And you're bored with it?

— Yes. I decided to stay put at the dacha.

— Where's your dacha?

— Out on the Yaroslavsky road.

— Whereabouts?

— In Pravda. There's nothing much there. Of course, it's nice and near, but there's nothing much to do...

— Live with your parents?

— Not now, I used to.

— And now?

— My grandmother died, so I've got her room.

— In a communal flat?

— Yes.

— What's it like?

— Oh, fine. The neighbours are decent, and it's right in the centre of town.

— It's fine if you've got nice neighbours...

— Yes... So, I'll just get changed if that's alright?

— Of course, feel free...

— It's so nice and warm...what a good big bathroom...did your ex-husband put in these nice tiles too?

— Yes.

— That's quite something. Master of so many arts...

— Ah, not really...

— So...here's your dressing gown. Thanks so much.

— You're welcome...

— It's so cosy here, I don't really feel like moving...

— Well, stay then! Have a cup of tea. It's still pouring out there anyway...

— You're terribly kind...but I'm sure you've got better things to do. I've just barged in...

— If I had better things to do I wouldn't've let you in in the first place...

— Well, that makes sense I suppose...

— Come and sit in the kitchen.

— Thanks...

— So is it Yugoslav ones you're queuing for, Vadim?

— No, that's the whole point—they're English.

— Oh...then I take it all back.

— I'd never have bothered if they'd just been Yugoslav.

— And they've given everyone numbers, have they?

— Yes.

— So what number are you?

— Oh, about two hundred and fiftieth.

— Wow, you've got a fair way to go...

— You call that a long way?! There were a good two thousand in that queue!

— You serious?

— Yeah, they're all sitting in the yards along the street.

— Uh-huh...sit yourself down, I'll just put the kettle on...

— You know something, that hair-style really suits you. I meant to tell you straight away.

— Does it really?

— M'm, honest. It's perfect for you.

— I was wishing I hadn't had it cut.

— No no, it's cute.

— Have they set up their stall out there in the street?

— Yes. They've put an awning up next to the shop and parked the vans alongside.

— So they must've called a halt in the meantime.

— Why, d'you reckon?

— Well they're not going to stand there in this rain are they? Everything'd get soaked.

— But they've got an awning up.

— Much use that is! Just look at that rain. The whole queue's disappeared.

— They're all in the doorways...

— Cigarette?

— Thanks...

— I keep trying to give up.

— Don't, it suits you. I like the cigarette holder.

— Ivory. Someone gave it to me not long ago.

— It's really pretty... allow me...

— *Merci*...

— Do you like cactuses?

— Love them. Well actually it's just lately I've had this thing about them.

— How come?

— I read that poem of Voznesensky's about cactuses. You know the one?

— Oh yeah... I remember...

— D'you like Voznesensky?

— I used to, a lot, but I've gone off him a bit...

— He's my favourite poet.

— He's a real master, no doubt about that...

— I can't stand Yevtushenko, but I absolutely adore Voznesensky.

VLADIMIR SOROKIN

— I don't think anyone likes both of them. You either like Voznesensky or you like Yevtushenko—it's the one or the other.
— I'm not denying Yevtushenko's got talent, but you know... always having an eye out for which way the wind blows ...that's what I can't stand...
— Well, he's a great show-off, of course.
— Exactly.
— Although he's written some decent things too. Like—what's that one—"The white snows are falling"...
— Well, of course. But Voznesensky's pure gold, he has such integrity, always strikes the right note. That's real poetry for you.
— Yeah...and he's so subtle describing feelings.
— His love poems are wonderful.
— M'm, I remember... "she lay there like a lake"...
— Do you like Tarkovsky?
— Yes. The patriarch.
— What about Samoilov?
— M'm, I like Samoilov too. "The forties, fateful, troubled times, times of gunpowder..."
— Great poet, isn't he?
— Terrific. And a very modest person too.
— What, do you know him?
— No, but a friend of mine does. He likes his drink, though, that's the only thing. But he's really down-to-earth, not standoffish at all. And a first-class mind, fantastically erudite...
— Sometimes I feel Samoilov's even closer to my heart than Tarkovsky.
— Tarkovsky's more refined, of course, more meditative, whereas Samoilov likes to take flight: he soars into the air like Pushkin...
— Exactly.
— I heard him a couple of times at the University. He reads his stuff very well.

— Does he?

— M'm. Restrained. Powerful...

— I heard Voznesensky a couple of times too. Once at the Polytechnic, and once at Tchaikovsky Hall.

— And how was he?

— Fantastic! I was so overcome, I clapped and cried like a little girl. He read to the accompaniment of the organ.

— Bach, was it?

— I think so. But imagine! Such power. "Let this time be wreathed..." It made me go all hot and cold...

— Yes, he can really get to you...

— He's brilliant...ah, the kettle's boiling...

— What are those little figurines called, I can never remember.

— What, those? They're Gzhel china.

— Oh, yes. Gzhel. Very pretty.

— I collect them.

— I've got a lion like that at home, made of the same stuff. I'll give it to you—don't have any use for it myself.

— Thanks very much.

— Be nice to add to your collection...

— We'll just let it brew...

— Lyuda...d'you mind if I call you Lyuda?

— I told you to straight away, didn't I?

— Do you like Bull's Blood, Lyuda?

— What, the wine? Yes, it's nice enough— why?

— Then I'll just run and get some at the shops. I saw they had some today...

— You're too late, I'm afraid.

— How come?

— Look at the clock behind you.

— What! It's past seven! That late!

— Anyhow, you can't go running out in this rain.

— God, what a series of disasters it's been today...

— Don't fret. I don't have any Bull's Blood, but there's some

Hungarian Vermouth ... if you'd just move a bit ... there ...
You open it ...

— Beautiful bottle.

— Here—these ones are nicer to drink from.

— Ah, yes ... what pretty glasses ...

— Ri-ight ... jam ... bread ... if you'd get the butter out of
there ...

— Uh-huh. Here you are ...

— Would you like something a bit more solid, Vadim? I wouldn't
mind a bite to eat myself.

— Well, just a bite, why not ...

— All I've got is fried potatoes.

— Wonderful. Potatoes, potatoes, ah de-li-cious potatoes ...

— Like them do you?

— M'm. Much tastier than meat, I always think.

— You're right. I'd like to give up eating meat as well.

— Look how low those clouds are.

— M'm ...

— What kind of stone is that in your ring, eh, Lyuda?

— Oh, it's just an ordinary turquoise.

— It's a beautiful ring.

— D'you like it?

— M'm, very much ...

— Ooh, stop, stop ... you'll make me drunk ...

— Ah, come on, it's very light.

— Right. Half the frying pan each, okay?

— Fantastic.

— I think we're all set ...

— All set. Everything's wonderful, Lyuda. I tell you what, why
don't we drink to the joy of unexpected meetings? There
aren't so many joys in life, after all. So, long may it last. To
our meeting.

— Alright then ... to our meeting ...

— ....

— ....mm, tasty...............

— Delicious wine.

— Have some sausage.

— Thanks. Let me give you ...

— That's enough, that's enough, Vadim ... thanks ... help yourself to some ....

— ....terrific potatoes...............

— ....Still pouring down ....it's incredible...........

— Mm ...yum yum ... these spuds are really tasty.........

— I put lots of herbs in, that's all ....

— ....uh-huh.....mmm......

— ....

— ....mmm...............

— May I?

— Just a drop...............

— Let's drink to you now, Lyuda. Your health.

— Thank you.

— ....wonderful Vermouth....

— ....brr.....

— Don't you like it?

— No, no, I do, I was just ....

— ....You're a marvellous cook, Lyuda.......
mmm.........

— *Merci*......Do eat up the sausage.....

— Thank you...............mmm.......

— ....

— ....

— ....

— ....mmm...."And outside the window it's raining. It's raining night and day..."

— Who was it wrote that?

— Your much-despised Yevtushenko.

— No, are you kidding?

— Uh-huh.

— Must have been one of his early ones. He used to be quite good.

— Yes....

— ....well, that's it then.....let's have a cup of tea....

— Can I help you?

— No no....I'll just............there.........

— What a fantastic day I've had...

— Yeah?

— Uh-huh. One moment I'm standing in some crazy queue being pushed around and waiting for God knows what. Next thing I know I'm sitting here drinking wine with a charming woman.

— Come on, don't exaggerate. Give me your cup.

— I'm not exaggerating. Some philosopher or other—Plato it was, I think—said it was worse to underestimate one's own beauty than to overestimate it...

— Haha...

— You know, you remind me incredibly of someone I once knew...

— Who?

— Oh...it was years and years ago...

— But who was she?

— We were students together.

— And? Is that too weak for you?

— No no, it's fine...We were in love, that's all.

— Well, I'm older than you, so it can't have been me.

— You're very like her. Really very alike...

— I don't want to look like some silly schoolgirl! Every woman is unique.

— Of course, of course...no, it was just...I was just reminded...

— There, there...have a biscuit...

— Thanks. Another little drop?

— I'm tipsy already, Vadim...

— Go on, just a tiny bit?

— Well, okay, just a drop...that's enough, that's enough!

— To your eyes. To your lovely brown eyes.

— Come on, why are we drinking to me the whole time?! Let's drink to your success as a journalist.

— No no, to your eyes.

— Goodness, the things you think up...

— To your eyes...

— To your success...

— To hell with my success. To your eyes...

— Okay, if you insist...............ooh...

— ....

— That's it. Now put the bottle away before it does any more mischief...

— Don't you like it?

— It's awfully strong.

— Very well, very well, your word is my command...though I must admit I would've liked...

— What?

— No, you'll be offended...

— What?

— No no...nothing...

— Go on Vadim, what was it?

— Well, I was just going to suggest we drink the special toast ...to saying '*tu*.' You know, link arms for *Bruderschaft*...

— For *Bruderschaft*?

— Yes.

— Hahaha! Why on earth?

— There, see, I told you you wouldn't want to...

— Who says I don't want to? Sure, if you like.

— Really?

— Yes, of course. But just a drop for me...purely symbolic...

— Okay...there...just a bit...

— Why did you suddenly decide...?

— Because I like you very much.

— Ooh, Vadim, you really are . . .

— No, I mean it.

— You've been standing a bit too long in the heat, that's all . . .

— The heat's got nothing to do with it.

— What a laugh though, really!

— It may be a laugh for you, but it isn't for me . . . Okay, shall we drink?

— I've forgotten the ritual . . . we link arms, do we?

— Yes. You stand here, and I'll go here. Then I put my arm through yours.

— Okay . . . the things people think up . . .

— And now we drink.

— Bit difficult . . .

— Down the hatch . . . .

— . . . . ooh . . .

— And now say '*tu*' to me.

— *Tu.*

— And I'll say '*tu*' to you. You're the most fascinating woman in the whole of Moscow.

— Hahaha! I think you better have some tea, Vadim.

— You've forgotten the '*tu*'!

— Sorry, I didn't mean . . . I just meant drink up your tea.

— That's more like it. Shall I pour some for you?

— Just a drop.

— Delicious tea. Indian?

— Yes. You know the packets with the little elephants?

— Aaah, yes . . .

— I keep my elephants in that little tin there.

— That pretty one?

— Uh-huh.

— But tell me, Lyuda, do you really live on your own?

— No.

— So who do you live with then?

— With Kulka.

— Who's that?

— My best friend.

— Girlfriend?

— Uh-huh. My most loyal companion. She's out on the balcony now.

— What d'you mean, who is she?

— My cat.

— Oh, Jesus... but why's she called Kulka?

— My grandmother had a cat called that, so I just gave her the same name.

— Funny name. Kulka....

— I don't know, I like it.

— Won't she get wet out there on the balcony?

— We've got a proper verandah, didn't you notice? It's glassed over.

— I didn't see.

— It's my pride and joy.

— I don't have any balcony at all.

— Ah, you'll survive.

— Is the rain easing off?

— Looks like it...

— Shouldn't think I'll be able to buy today in any case...

— I bet the salesgirls have all run off.

— Yes... anyhow, it's so nice here.

— D'you like it?

— Mmm. It's so long since I've been anywhere really cosy...

— Ah, what a hard life we lead!

— Seriously, you've got beautiful eyes...

— Back on that one, are we...

— I could gaze and gaze at them... forever...

— Like some more tea?

— No-o. Listen, have you got any music?

— I've got a record-player. The tape-recorder's broken.

— Shall we have a dance?

— Why, d'you like dancing?

— I used to once upon a time, but I haven't danced for years. Shall we?

— Okay, sure...Though all my records are a bit dated I'm afraid...

— Ah, who cares...it was a wonderful meal, thank you.

— It's over here.

— Stereo, is it?

— Uh-huh.

— Perfect...right...wow, what a pile of them...Mireille Mathieu...some Czech or other...

— He's a saxophonist.

— Right...hey, why d'you say you've only got old stuff. Here's Joe Dassin.

— Well, that's about the only one...

— Shall we put him on?

— Okay.

— Right...that's on...is this how...?

— Uh-huh, and then that little lever...

— Right...great...there we are. He's a brilliant singer, isn't he?

— M'm. Too bad he died.

— May I invite you, Lyudmila Konstantinovna?

— Listen, you know what...Could you go out for just one second?

— Why, what's up?

— You'll see in a minute.

— Okay...

— I'll literally be a minute...

— Feel free. I'll just make a phone call in the meantime.

— Do, the phone's in the kitchen.

— Uh-huh...right...two, o, o, two, o, three...two...o...three...uh-huh...Mum? Hello. I did try and ring. Honest. I just couldn't get through...uh-huh....yes. Of course...

uh-huh . . . It's going to take ages. Of course. Me? So what?
What's it got to do with me? . . . I've no idea . . . No . . . Why're
you so upset? It's not my fault is it? Yes, yes, of course . . .
No . . . Well, no, of course not . . . No, Mum, Volodya's got
nothing to do with it. Seriously. Absolutely. No, you're just
imagining it . . . yes. Yes! I . . . tomorrow, probably. Late tomorrow. Well I've got nothing much else to do anyway . . . of
course . . . uh-huh. Okay, say hello to . . . uh-huh . . . uh-
huh . . . bye . . .

— Vadim!
— Yes?!
— I'm waiting.
— I'm coming . . . my God . . . Who's this!
— Hahaha!
— What magic! What have you done!
— Nothing!
— But it's fantastic! What a dress! Straight out of the movies!
— Hahaha!
— Fantastic! Before such a dazzling spectacle a man can
only . . . go down on bended knee . . . there . . . and beg for
your hand . . .
— Hahaha!
— So may I invite you now?
— Where's your white tail coat?
— It's being flown in from Paris as we speak! It'll be here by the
end of the dance . . . May I?
— You're a really funny guy, you know that?
— No more than most.
— My ex had no sense of humour at all.
— Yes, well, you get people like that.
— He'd get upset at the slightest thing.
— A difficult case, eh?
— I had to translate everything for him.
— Translate the jokes?! Hahaha!

— May sound funny to you, but I was just miserable...ooh, my head's spinning...you've got me completely drunk...

— I love this next one. It's beautiful, isn't it?

— Mmm. So tender... tara-ra-ra-raa-raa-raaam...

— See how quickly it's got dark...

— Yes... tara-ra-ra-raa-raam...

— You know...I reckon this is the loveliest evening I've had for the last five years.

— Really?

— Mmm...

— Why?

— Because... because...

— Vadim... Vadim...

— My darling...you're gorgeous...

— Vadim... Vadim

— ....you're love....ly...

— ...Vadim...why...ah...

— ....

— ....Vadim......... really.....

— ....gorgeous...............

— ....don't...............

— ....

— ....Vadim...............

—

— Mmm...............what...............ah......

— ....

— ....

— Mm, may I?

— Completely dark...

— You're lovely...lovely...

— Vadim...but we don't know each other at all...

— ....lovely....your lovely neck...

— ....Vadim......... Vadim...

— ....Lyudochka...

— ....
— .... it's so nice with you ...
— Vadim ....
— ....
— You shouldn't .... sweetheart .... why ....
— ....
— Vadik .... aah ....
— ....
— Baby .... you shouldn't .....
— ....
— It comes off this way ....
— ....
— Wait, I'll draw the blinds.
— You're lovely.
— Take the cover off ...
— Come to me ...
— Can you unfasten me ... it's got caught ...
— M'm ..... my petal ....
— God .... damned dress ...
— There ...
— Just a bit more ...
— Darling ...
— Ooh ...
— ....
— .... aah .... my baby ...
— ....
— .... baby .... darling ....
— .... aaah .....
....
— Sweetheart ....
— ....
— Ooh ...
— Haaa ...
— Aahh ...

— Haaa...
— Ahh...
— Haaa....
— Ahh...ba...by...
— Haaa...
— Aahh...
— Haaa...
— Aaah...oh...
— Haaa....
— Ooaah...ah...
— Ha...
— Aaah...sweet...heart...
— Haa...
— Aah...ooh...
— Haaa...
— Aah...Va...di...mmm...
— Haa...
— Aaah.....
— Haaa...
— Aaah....my...ba..by....
— Haaa....
— Aaah......
— Haa....
— Ah....
— Haaa....
— Ah...
— Haaa....
— Aaah....
— Haa....
— Ah...Ah...
— Haaa....
— Aaah....
— Haaa...dar...ling...

— Aah....my...dear...my...
— Haa...
— Aaaa!
— Haaa...
— Aaah...
— Haaa...
— Aaah....aaa...aaaa!
— Haa....
— Aaah.....
— Haaa....my...pre...cious....
— Aaah.....
— Haaa...!
— Aaah.....
— Haa!
— Aah....
— Haa!
— Ah....
— Ha!
— Ah...
— Ha!
— Ah.
— Ha!
— Ah.
— Ha!
— Ah.
— Ha!
— Ah.
— Ha!
— Ah.
— Ha!
— Ah.
— Ha!
— Ah.

— Ha!

— Ah.

— Ha!

— Aaaah ... oh ...

— Ha!

— Aaah ...

— Haa!

— Aaah ...

— Haa!

— Ah.

— Ha!

— Aaah .....

— Ha!

— Aaah ...

— Ha! Ooah!

— Aaah ... my ... dar ... ling ...

— Ha!

— Aaaa ... aaaa! Aa! Aaaa! Oh! Darling! Aaaaa! Aaaa!

— Ha!

— Aaaa! Aaaa! Oh! Aaah ... darling! Aaaa! Aaaa!

— Ha!

— Aaaa ..... aaah .... aaaa ....

— Ha! Aaaa .... oooh .... oooaaaah ...... love ......
yeeeessss ....

— Oooh .... ooo .... darling ...... baby .... aaah ....

— Aaaa ... aaa ... lovely .... lovely .... aaaa ....

— Ooooh ... little sunshine ... oooh ...

— Aaaaa ... aaa ... aaa ... love you ....

— Ooooh ..... adore you ....

— Darling ...

— Precious.

— Sweetheart ...

— My treasure ... my little boy ...

— Lovely .....

— My baby...

— Your breasts are simply wonderful...

— Like them?

— Who wouldn't...

— My baby...

— You're gorgeous.

— Ooh...we were lying right on the blanket...pull it away...

— Uh-huh...

— Wait a moment, darling, I'll be right back...

— You're a goddess...what a figure! like Cleopatra.

— I tell you what, come in here with me, let me wash you...

— God...I must be dreaming...

— Come here...

— Darling...

— Climb in...put the plug in...

— Ooh...it's cold...

— It'll get warm in a second...

— Ooh! What a tap!

— It won't take a minute to fill...move up.

— It's a real waterfall...oooh...

— Give me the soap...it's just there....

— Uh-huh...

— If you kneel....

— My darling...

— Hold onto me...

— And then can I wash you?

— Of course...there...sweet little sausage...

— My darling...

— He's worked so hard...poor little thing...

— Ooh!...

— Watch out, don't drown me.

— It's a bit hot...

— Turn on the cold a bit more...

— Uh-huh...there...that's better...

— So little...so sweet....

— Mmm...

— And now down here...all soft and cosy...

— Aaah....

— And now your little bottom...little sweaty bottom....

— Mm...your hands are so tender...

— There we are...there...

— Aaaah...

— And now here...and here...

— What's that little scar, Lyuda?

— Some glass fell on me...there...

— Darling...

— There...now we're all nice and clean...

— Let me do you now.

— Turn off the water, it's overflowing...

— Uh-huh...

— You're really well-built...such a muscly feller...

— Listen...ooh, lovely...

— Baby...

— Gorgeous...

— D'you like them?

— Fantastic...look how soft and slippery.

— They're all yours, darling...

— How about doing it here, ah?

— Oooh...what's this I see? Who have we got here?

— Let's do it, darling...

— Three people stood on the bridge: him, her, and his little...

— Come on, let's, come on...

—What, in the bath! We can't...it won't work...I'll get out...

— My Cleopatra...

— Here, like this...

— Come a bit lower...there...

— Ooh...darling...ooh...

— Haaa...

— Aaah...
— Haaa...
— Aaah.....
— Haaa...
— Aaah.....
— Haa!
— Aaah....ba...by...ba...by.
— Haaa....
— Aaah.....
— Haaa....
— Aaah.....
— Haaa!
— Aaah....aaa....
— Haaa! Dar...ling...
— Aaah.....
— Haaa!
— Aaah....aaa...
— Haaa!
— Aaah.....
— Haaa!
— Ah....
— Ha....
— Aaaah.....
— Haaa!
— Ooooh! Aaa....
— Haaa...
— Aaah.....
— Haa...
— Aah.....
— Haa...
— Aaah.....
— Haaa! Oooo...unnn...
— Aaah.....
— Haaa!

— Oooh...go...on...a...gain...
— Ha!
— Oh....
— Ha!
— Aaaah....
— Ha!
— Ah....
— Ha! Oh...oh...
— Aaaaah.....
— Haaa.
— Aaah.....
— Haaa.
— Aaah.....
— Haaa.
— Aaah....sweet...heart...
— Ha!
— Ah.....
— Ha!
— Ah!
— Ha!
— Ah!
— Ha!
— Ahhh....ooo...
— Ha!
— Ooooh...ah....
— Ah!
— Oooh....
— Aha!
— Aaaaa....
— Aha!
— Ooooo...
— Aha!
— Ooooo....
— Aha!

— Ah . . . .
— Aha!
— Oh . . . ba . . . by . . . .
— Aha!
— Aaaa . . . .
— Aha!
— Aaaa . . . .
— Aha!
— Aaaah . . . .
— Aha!
— Ooooh . . . ooh!
— Aha!
— Oh . . . oh . . . .
— Aha!
— Oh . . . .
— Aha . . . .
— Mooore . . . aaa . . .
— Aha!
— Oh . . . .
— Aha!
— Aaaa . . . . .
— Aha!
— Aaa . . . .
— Oh!
— Aaaa . . . .
— Oh!
— Aaa . . . .
— O!
— Aaaa . . .
— Hah!
— Mo . . . ore . . . .
— Hah!
— Ooooh . . . .
— Hah!

— Aaaah . . . .

— Hah!

— Aaa! Aaaa! Oh! Aaaa! Aaaa! Oh! Aaaa! Aaaaa! Aaaaaaaa!

— Hah!

— Aaaa!

— Hah!

— Aaaaaaaaaai!

— Hah!

— Aaaaai!

— Haaaa!

— Aaaai!

— Haaa!

— Aai!

— Ha!

— Ai!

— Ha!

— Aaa . . . . oh . . . darling . . . . I can't . . . .

— Ha!

— Oh . . . I . . . caaaan't . . . .

— Ha!

— Oh . . . . God . . . .

— Ha!

— Oh . . . .

— Ha!

— Oooh . . . .

— Ha!

— Ooh . . . .

— Ha!

— Ooh . . . .

— Ha . . . uuuuuunnnnnnnnnnhhhh . . . ammmmmmmmaaaaa
. . . . oommmmmm . . . . mmmmmmm . . . .

— My . . . ra . . . bb . . . it . . . my . . .

— Mmmmmmmm . . . . . oooommmmm . . . . mmmmmmm . . . . .
ommm . . . . oaaaammmm.

— Ba...by...

— Mmmmmmm....

— Sweet...heart....

— Mmmm....

— Baby...

— Ooooh....

— Baby...

— Ooh....

— My baby. So nice with you...

— Ooh....

— Darling...

— Ooh...slipped out...there....ah...

— Mind you don't drown...

— Oooof.....too much....

— Move a bit...ooh! It's all coming out...

— Aaaah....you're an amazing woman...ooooh.

— My little baby....

— Oooh....what bliss...lie down here....

— Don't get my hair wet...oop-la...oh!

— So nice...

— My baby...

— Shall we turn the light out and go to sleep?

— In the water?

— Uh-huh...

— Don't be silly...we'll get completely sodden. Your little cannon will come unstuck...

— Hahaha....

— Have I drowned you...

— Not yet...

— Nice roomy bath I've got, eh?

— I'll say...

— Tired, my little worker?

— Done in...can't lift a finger...

— Got tired so quick?

— Aaaah . . . .
— 'Course, you were standing all that time in the queue . . .
poor baby. . . .
— And now I'm slowly dissolving . . .
— Want a drink?
— M'm, just a drop.
— You lie here and soak, I'll be back in a moment . . . oops
. . . give me a hand . . . .
— There you go . . . .
— That's it . . . .
— You should be a Hollywood star with breasts like that . . . .
— They'll pass, will they?
— Gorgeous . . .
— Not bad for forty-two.
— What, are you forty-two?
— Uh-huh . . .
— I'd never have guessed . . .
— Can't believe it myself . . .
— And you've got such a pretty ass . . . lovely and round . . . .
— Passes muster as well, does it . . . right, I'll just nip and get . . . .
— Can you put some cold water with the Vermouth?
— Okay . . .
— Ooh . . . where's the . . .
— Vadim! D'you want some tea?
— No! God . . . the acoustics . . .
— It's nice and hot!
— No thanks!
— As you like . . . just a sec . . . here . . .
— Tara-ra-tar-ra . . . tara-ra-ra-raaam . . .
— What?
— Nothing . . .
— What did you say, darling?!
— Nothing!
— Aaah . . . . I'll bring you . . . here . . .

— Mm, wonderful . . . aren't you freezing?

— Not yet.

— . . . mmm . . . nice and cold . . . terrific . . .

— Drink up and let's get into bed.

— Don't you want to get in the bath?

— Not now, maybe later. Let's lie down for a bit.

— . . . . thank you, my darling . . . .

— You're welcome. Come on . . . climb out . . .

— Give me your hand . . . there . . .

— Let me dry your back . . .

— That's a pretty towel.

— It's Chinese. You can't get them like that any more.

— Thanks . . . that's nice . . . hurry up then, into bed . . .

— Ooh . . .

— What's the matter?

— Kulka's scratching . . . I'll just let her in . . .

— Go on then . . . I can't see where . . .

— There it is . . . straight ahead.

— Ah yes . . . ooh, how lovely . . . the nuptial couch . . . splendid . . .

— Puss puss, are you cold? In you go . . . .

— Aren't you too hot with a warm blanket in summer, Lyuda?

— No, it's nice . . .

— There's only one pillow . . .

— Hold on, I'll get another . . .

— No, it's stopped.

— You don't have a TV?

— It broke, I'm having it repaired.

— I see . . . .

— Here's a pillow . . .

— Come and lie down.

— Ooh . . . brrr . . . warm me up . . . .

— Come closer.

— Mmm . . . you're so nice and warm . . .

— You're frozen . . . my little girl . . . .

— You're so warm . . . you've got such lovely soft skin . . .

— You too . . . .

— Have you ever been married, Vadim?

— Never officially.

— Why not?

— She just didn't want to.

— You didn't have any children?

— No. She kept having abortions.

— Did you break up a long time ago?

— Yes, six years ago now . . .

— I've only been living on my own this last year.

— Were you together long?

— Twelve years.

— That's quite a time . . . snuggle up . . . there . . .

— And what was she like?

— Meaning?

— Well, was she nice?

— Yes.

— What did she do?

— Microbiologist.

— Was she the first woman you had?

— No, of course not . . . .

— Who was your first then?

— Oh, a student. Lived in the hostel . . . what about you?

— He was a student too. When we were doing practicals . . .

— So, have you warmed up?

— Uh-huh . . .

— Your hair's lovely and soft . . . lovely . . .

— My baby . . .

— Aaah . . . shit . . . .

— What's up?

— Nothing. I was just remembering the damned queue . . . shit . . . .

— Why, what's the matter?

— Queued up all that time for nothing, as it turns out...

— Were you really doing it for your friend?

— No, not really...it was for me....

— So you were telling fibs, you liar...

— Still, they're American ones...you know...

— Yes, I know...you've got such big muscles...

— I thought I'd get them today...

— Nice firm tummy as well—look at that. Ooh, and what's this now...

— And I spent last night sleeping on a bench...

— Poor little thing...how could you...listen, why are balls always colder than cocks?

— I don't know....

— You're the other way round...so warm...

— You're nice and warm in there too...

— Put your hand here...

— So tender....

— Kiss me....

— ....

— ...darling.....

— Your lips....so soft and tender.

— Ooh...all hard again...how lovely...

— My tender one....

— Ooh....what a lovely big one....

— Darling....

— Vadik...

— Aaaah....mmmm....

— Take the blanket off....

— My darling...

— Move up a bit higher...

— Ooh, why, Lyuda...ooh...

— ....

— Oooo....nn...oh....aah....

— ...spread your knees...
— Lyuda...what are you...I'm not worthy...oooh... Lyulochka...ah...oooh...lovely...ooh...my darling... aaaah...nnh...my...dear...my...precious...Ooh...ooh ...aaah...Lyudochka...Lyudochka...Lyudochka...Lyu- dochka...darling...you're gorgeous...my darling...oooh ...I can't stand it...sweetheart...I'm going to die...ah ...Oh...my...love...oooh...aaaaaah...my darling... I'm going to die...I'm going to die...Lyuda...I can't ...come quickly...Come quickly...quickly...Lyud.... let's do it from behind...
— As you like...darling...
— Wait...there...uh-huh....
— Knocked me out....
— Higher up, higher up...aaah...tastes so sweet, like an or- ange...
— Aaah...
— Aaaah...
— Ha...
— Aha...
— Ha...
— Aaah...
— Haa...
— Aaah...
— Haa...
— Aaaaah...
— Haa...
— Aaah...
— Haa...
— Aaaaah...
— Haaa...
— Aaaaaah...aaaaaah...ba...by...my...ba...be...
— Haaa...
— Aaaaaah...

— Haaa...
— Aaaah...
— Haaa...
— Aaaah...
— Haa...
— Aaaah...
— Haaa...
— Aaah...oh...aaah...ba...by...
— Ha...
— Aaaah...
— Haaah...
— Aaah...
— Haah...
— Aaaah...
— Haaah...
— Aaaah...
— Haah...
— Aaaaaah...ooh...ooh...o!!
— Hah!
— Ah...
— Hah!
— Aaah...
— Hah!
— Aaah...
— Hah!
— Aaaah...
— Hah!
— Aaaah...
— Hah!
— Aaa...
— Hah!
— Aaaa...
— Hah!
— Aaaa...

— Hah!

— Aaaaa...

— Hah!

— Aaaa...

— Hah!

— Aaaa...

— Hah!

— Aaaa...

— Hah!

— Aaaaa...

— Hah!

— Ooh...ba...by...ba...by!

— Hah!

— Ooooh...

— Hah!

— Ooooh...

— Hah!

— Aaah...

— Hah!

— Aaah...

— Hah!

— Ooooh! Ooh! Ooooooh! Aaaaa! Aaaaaa! Aaaaaaaaaai! Aaaaa! Aaaaaai!

— Hah!

— Ooooooh! Oooooooh! Baby! Oh! Can't bear it! Oh! Oh! Aaaaaaa! Aaaaaaai!

— Hah!

— Ooooooh!

— Hah!

— Oooooo...can't ...stand....it...

— Ha!

— Ooooh!

— Ha!

— Ooooooh...

— Ha!

— Oooooh...can't...bear...

— Hah!

— Oooooh...

— Haaaa!

— Ooh! Ooh! Ooh! Oooooh! Aaaaai! Aaaaaai! Aaaaa! Aaa!
Aaaaaa! Aaaaaa! Aaaaa!

— Hah!

— Aaaa!

— Hah!

— Aaaaai!

— Hah!

— Aaai!!

— Hah!

— Aaaai!!

— Hah!

— Aaai! Aaaai!!

— Haah!

— Ooooh...

— Hah!

— Aaaa...

— Hah!

— Va...dim...

— Hah!

— Va...dim...

— Ha!

— Va...dik!

— Ha!

— Vadi...k...dar...ling...

— Ha...aaaah...unnnnnnnnh...uuuuuuuuh...aaaaaaaaaah!
...uuuh! aaa!...aaaaaa...

— Dar...ling...

— Aaaaam...ammmmmmmm...daaaarling...mmmmm...

— Baby...

— Daaarling...mmmm...
— Vadik...precious...
— Ooommmmmmm.....ommmm....
— My own baby....
— Ooh...you're lovely...
— You're lovely too...
— Knocked out...ooh...done in...darling...
— My baby...my little worker...
— Out of this world...ooh...aah....
— I won't be a sec.
— Aaaah...mmmmm.

— Vadik! Vadik! What, are you asleep?
— Ah? God...just drifted off...ooh....
— My baby. You tired?
— No, just...sort of trance...ooh...
— Me too, you know, I'm sort of...you're so dynamic.
— I was just in a sort of trance...
— Oooh, you're so warm. My darling...
— Wooow...you're a very sexy woman...
— *Merci.*
— Ooh...hold me....
— You're tired, my precious...
— Tired...

— You go to sleep, my sweetheart . . . sleep . . .

— You too . . . don't go away . . . darling . . .

— I'm here with you. I'm here . . . .

— Ooh . . . fantastic . . . just like a dream . . .

— Sleep . . . . my baby . . . .

— Ooooaaaah . . . kiss . . . . .

— . . . . little one . . . .

— Ooh . . . aaah . . . waaah . . .

VLADIMIR SOROKIN

VLADIMIR SOROKIN

VLADIMIR SOROKIN

VLADIMIR SOROKIN

VLADIMIR SOROKIN

VLADIMIR SOROKIN

VLADIMIR SOROKIN

THE QUEUE

— Ooh...whew...ooh...Lyuda, what's the time? Lyuda! Lyuda!

— What's the...?

— Lyuda! Time...what time is it?

— I don't know...clock's there...why d'you wake up... ooh....

— Where...where's the clock...it's nearly eight?!

— What's the big hurry....

— Roll call...damn...I completely forgot about roll call.... probably had one during the night...Shit! where are my underpants?

— Somewhere there...

— I'm late...gone and missed the queue...must be cracked...

— What are you...God...at this hour of the morning....

— There they are...and I kept thinking....

— Hold on...Vadim...

— What d'you mean, hold on! My queue's out there!

— Wait a moment, stupid! Lie down!

— Are you crazy or what? You should've reminded me yesterday! Where the hell are my trousers?

— Come here!

— What?! I'm late!

— You're not late for anything.

— Why not?

— Because we're not selling today.

— Who's we?

— Us. The workers at the Moskva stores.

— What's the Moskva stores got to do with it?

— What it's got to do with is that we organised the sale... ooooaawaah...and today we've got stock-taking in every department...

— So?

— So nothing. Go to sleep. And the day after tomorrow I'll take you to the depot and you'll get to choose whichever you want...

— Hold on...I thought you said you were an economist?

— I was joking, darling. Sorry. I studied at a trade college, I never went to an institute. My husband was against it...

— Where do you work then?

— I told you, at the Moskva stores.

— What do you do there?

— I'm the head of our department.

— What about the queue? I don't understand...there are people queuing out there....

— So let them queue. They'll have to wait till the day after tomorrow.

— What, do you...d'you have something to do with the queue then?

— Yes, yes, yes! God, you're slow! It's us that's selling, us! My girls and me! It's just that I left early yesterday to escape the rain.

— So it was you up there, was it?

— Yes, yes, me...lie down....

— God...but this is...!

— Lie down, Vadim. You were screwing me the whole damn night, and now you won't let me sleep.

— So you mean they aren't selling anything right now?

— No, no! All the goods are going back to the store till the day after tomorrow...we didn't manage to sell them before stock-taking...there are about three hundred left.

— And are they really American?

— Yes...Are you going to lie down or not?!

— I am, I am...But listen, if you've got stock-taking, why are you at home?

— I'm on sick leave.

VLADIMIR SOROKIN

— Pretend, you mean?
— Of course...let them stew in their own juice...they can sort it out....
— My lovely warm Lyuda...aaah...move over...
— I meant to tell you yesterday but I forgot...
— Why did you lie to me and say you were an economist?
— Oh, just...I saw straight away you were a highbrow type... you know....
— You silly...what does it matter...my darling...
— Put your arms round me...
— You funny little thing...God, what an amazing summer... so many strange things....
— Ah, what can you do...it's all in the stars...
— Mm....
— Aaaaoooh...sleep, darling...when we get up, I'll make you some nice chicken tabaka...
— I'm asleep...
— Do you like chicken tabaka?
— Mm...
— Are you asleep?
— I'm asleep. I'm asleep...

AFTERWORD
Farewell to the Queue

An era can be judged by street conversations.

"Look, there's a line."

"What're they giving out?"

"Just get on it, then we'll find out."

"How much should I get?"

"As much as they'll give you."

This touching dialogue from the Brezhnev era should be etched on the stern granite of Lenin's mausoleum—in memory of the great era of socialist paradise. And if anyone were to think seriously about a monument to that period, I would suggest that the empty mausoleum (should Lenin's body ever be finally consigned to the earth) be filled with those deficit, prestige items for which Soviet citizens suffered such torments standing in line. American Lees and Levi Strauss jeans, Camel and Marlboro cigarettes, "spike" heel and platform shoes, "stocking" boots, cervelat sausage and salami, Sony and Grundig tape recorders, French perfume, Turkish sheepskin coats, muskrat hats, and Bohemian crystal—I can just see it all, under glass like the eidos of real socialism, lying in the triumphant half dark of the mausoleum. Every year, the number of people wanting to catch a glimpse of Lenin's stand-in would increase, so that decades later the line would be a unique, living relic of bygone days.... But enough about bygone days. Here we are—in the new, post-Communist era:

"Look, there's beef. And no line."

"I haven't got enough money. Let's buy potatoes instead."

Not all that long ago, Soviet people couldn't even have imagined such a scene, and it proved tremendously difficult to come to terms with it. The ordeal of the free market turned out to be more frightening than the Gulag, and more burdensome than the bloody war years, because it forced people to part with the oneiric space of collective slumber, forced them to leave the ideally balanced Stalinist cosmos behind. The steel hands of the world's first proletarian government, which carried us from cradle to grave, cracked and fell off. Along with them went all the familiar socialist ways: free education and medical care, the absence of unemployment, the irrelevance of money, and finally, an entire system of distribution. It turned out to be particularly agonizing to part with the latter. It was the living flesh that inhabited the rigid ideological armature of the government, it lubricated and cushioned people from the Party nomenclature apparatchiks, and it stimulated the black market, which brought Soviet people all sorts of small pleasures. Then, suddenly, everything, everything turned to dust. And the queue? That fantastic, many headed monster, the hallmark of socialism? Where has it gone, the monstrous Leviathan that wound entire cities in its motley coils? Where are the long hours of standing, the stirring shouts, the dramatic confrontations, the joyous trembling of the person at the head of the line?

In a catastrophically short time—just a couple of years—the line was dispersed and reborn as a crowd. It's probable that the queue is gone for good. Like everything epic that has plunged into the Lethe, it arouses interest. Not merely socio-ethnographic interest. One composer I know is seriously considering writing an opera titled *The Queue* in the style of a Russian epic: with mass scenes, choruses, a complex plot. Perhaps at the opening, many of the viewers, despite their own rich personal experience of standing in line, will ask the question: What was this thing after all, the queue?

Paradoxical as it may seem, the line was a purely Soviet phenomenon. Until the Bolsheviks came to power no such phenomenon had been observed in Russia. There are three events in Russian history that allow us to understand the phenomenon of the queue more fully. The first took place on May 18, 1896, on Khodynskoe Field near Moscow. In honor of the coronation of Nicholas II a public celebration was announced and it was promised that bags of gifts from the Tsar would be distributed. Each of these bags contained an enamel mug, a cloth, a link of sausage, a bottle of beer, some sugar, and spice cookies. Newspaper advertisements and word of mouth carried the news of the Tsar's gifts far beyond Moscow. The field was filled with people more than a day before the celebration. Night fell, and people kept arriving.

At dawn, according to the well-known writer and journalist Vladimir Giliarovsky, who witnessed the scene: "Khodynskoe Field resembled a huge barrel packed with herring, stretching all the way to the horizon, over which there hung a thick cloud of human breath." Whether by some sinister irony of fate or the stupidity of the organizers, the field was surrounded by ditches and fences that transformed it into an enormous trap: you could get in, but you couldn't get out. The booths where the gifts were to be distributed were clustered in one area. About six o'clock in the morning someone waved a hat. This was taken as a signal that the gifts were being handed out. The crowd moved toward the booths. A terrible crush ensued: people fell, they were trampled, they tumbled into the ditches, were crushed against fences. Giliarovsky, a man of extraordinary physical strength, known to bend horseshoes and coins with his bare hands, only just managed to break free of this hell, and fell into a deep faint. Altogether, more than two thousand people died on Khodynskoe Field.

The event itself is extraordinarily metaphorical and significant: a huge crowd accumulates in an enclosed space, consumes food in a frenzy, and crushes itself before the eyes of the young Tsar! It should be noted that the mass revolutionary movement began in Russia after the Khodynskoe tragedy. It is no exaggeration to say that a new type of object or metaphorical subject was born into Russian history that morning on Khodynskoe Field: the collective body. This body grew with each year, acquiring energy. Its actions against the Tsarist regime became more and more aggressive and decisive. The authorities tried to conduct negotiations with this body; they bribed it, surrounded it with troops, and finally shot at it, as happened on Bloody Sunday, January 9, 1905, when an enormous crowd in St. Petersburg set out toward the Winter Palace with a petition for the Tsar. In 1914 those same authorities tried to use its energy for military purposes, directing it against an external enemy. But the collective body's response was rather sluggish; in foreign fields, far away from the Motherland, it lost its energy, entropied. Having dissolved into molecules by 1917, it overran the capital only to gather itself into a raging fist and strike a crippling blow to the powers that be. The last two years of the Civil War didn't stop it, and by 1920 the collective body had come to power for good, inaugurating the era of the "Uprising Masses," which displayed to the world at large its astonishing ethics and aesthetics.

It was after the victory of the collective body that the phenomenon of the queue appeared in Russia with all its classic attributes: numeration (the person's number in line was usually written on the hand); the periodic roll call and ruthless elimination of anyone who stepped away for a moment; a strict hierarchy (those standing behind were supposed to obey those standing in front); the quantity of goods allotted per person (this was also decided collectively), etc.

The time of interminable lines began. People stood in line for everything—for bread, sugar, nails, news of an arrested husband, tickets to *Swan Lake*, furniture, Komsomol vacation tours. In communal apartments people waited in line for the toilet. In overcrowded prisons people queued up for a turn to lie down and sleep. According to statistics, Soviet citizens spent a third of each day standing in lines.

"We go to the lines like we go to our jobs!" my grandmother used to joke. The Russian word *sluzhba*, job or service, implies not only work (in an office, a factory, or, before the Revolution, for the gentry) but a church service. And in the Russian Orthodox Church there are no pews, people stand during the service.

"I stood through an all-nighter."*

"I stood three hours for butter."

The ambiguity of such dialogues is obvious. No, it was not only for butter and nails that people stood in endless lines. The queue was a quasi-surrogate for church. Through the act of standing up, standing up for, through, and in and on lines (i.e., in all senses of the word "to stand," *trans.*) regularly for several hours, people participated in a sort of ritual, after which, instead of the Eucharist and absolution of their sins, they received foodstuffs and manufactured goods.

The collective body was steadily ritualized by queues. It was taught order and obedience, and rendered maximally governable. At mass demonstrations, show trials, Party congresses, and soccer games the collective body was allowed to express the orgiastic side of its nature: it applauded stormily and raged, it shuddered with countless orgasms. But on ordinary workdays the line awaited it. Gray and boring, but inescapable, the line dissected the body into pieces, pacified and disciplined it, gave people time to think about the advantages of socialism and about the class struggle; and in the end they were rewarded with food and goods.

In essence, during the Stalin years the populace engaged in a

---

* The same sentence could be translated as "I stayed through the all-night mass," or "I stood in line all night."

daily rehearsal for the Line of all Lines, in which virtually the entire collective body would stretch itself out and in so doing mark the end of the stormy era of the "Uprising Masses." The occasion for such a line arose on March 5, 1953, when the heart of the People's Father and Great Empiricist of the Masses stopped beating.

For three days, Stalin's body lay on view in its coffin in the House of Unions in central Moscow so the people could say farewell. The enormous line to see Stalin stretched through half of the capital. Muscovites and pilgrims from cities and villages all over the country came in an endless stream. Russia had never seen such a queue.

Once again, as on Khodynskoe Field, the collective body was surrounded, this time by army trucks. On the last night a stampede began. Tears pouring from their eyes as they mourned their Leader, the crowd flattened people against the trucks, trampled them underfoot. No one knows exactly how many people perished that night, but corpses were taken away by the truckload.

The goal of the Stalinist era was achieved—the collective body organized itself into the Line of Lines, stood through it, and, having made a traditional sacrifice to the deceased leader, dissolved into obedient molecules. Stalin tranquilized the Russian people. The period of the "Tranquil Masses" began.

During the motley era of Khrushchev's Thaw, the ritual of standing in lines acquired definitive features, having cleansed itself of arbitrary individualism and non-canonic collective movements. During the reign of Brezhnev—the northern Buddha, as some called him—the line had already become a genuine trademark of developed socialism and occupied an honored place next to such profoundly symbolic phenomena as St. Basil's Cathedral, Russian caviar, the Russian soul, Lenin's mausoleum, and the Soviet military threat.

Like semiprecious stones polished by time, ritual phrases shone in all their sacred purity. No line could do without them:

"Comrades, who's last in line?"

"What are they giving out?"

"How much a head?"

"You weren't standing here!"

"I've been standing since five this morning!"

In the 1970s, the carefree days of "stagnation," people no longer stood for butter and sugar, which were in adequate supply thanks to the wise policies of détente and cheap Soviet oil. Instead, they waited in line for "imports": American jeans, German shoes, Italian knitwear. They waited happily, with humor, in a familial atmosphere that was even rather cozy. After an hour of togetherness waiting in line, the man in front of you in a leather cap with a tanned, friendly face might tell you stories of his dangerous work as a geologist in the far north, about a bear hunt that almost turned tragic, about the ecological problems of the northern rivers, about fantastical sunsets in the taiga and songs around the campfire with a guitar. The woman standing behind you, dressed in a colorful sweater, her eyes slightly swollen from tears, would begin with the standard phrase: "All men are the same," and then tell you about her divorce (which finally went through the day before yesterday) from her alcoholic husband, who shamelessly drank up her mother's life savings (an invalid of labor!) and her father's too (a hero of the battle of Stalingrad!). All of this seamlessly flowed into the roll call carried out by some decently dressed, slightly nervous pensioner, most likely a former lieutenant-colonel. An hour later, having paid the government a trivial sum, you joyfully hid the desired foreign-label item in your briefcase. . . .

But, unfortunately, *Tempora mutantur, et nos mutamur in illis.*

The twilight '80s arrived. The empire crawled slowly toward collapse. Every year, the provision of the collective body with essential goods worsened. The many headed caterpillar no longer wound its way waiting for Levi Strauss and Salamander shoes but for sausage and butter.

The hysterical era of perestroika began. The jokes and soulful confessions once heard in line dwindled. A morose readiness for new hardship appeared on faces. People expected endless queues, four-figure numbers on their hands, days and days of standing. Old people recalled the war years, the siege of Leningrad and its daily 125-gram bread ration, they shared their survival experiences. But what came crashing down on the collective body in the beginning of the 1990s turned out to be scarier than the Leningrad blockade.

It was the atom bomb of a market economy.

After its raucous explosion, people standing in lines discovered three terrible truths:

1. Money is real.
2. The people standing next to you in line have different abilities.
3. There are not 3 kinds of sausage, but 33. Or even 333.

The queue shuddered and began to waver.

Entrepreneurial citizens who wanted to open their own stores and sell sausage, rather than stand in line for it, immediately left its ranks. They were followed by those active citizens who wanted to make money in the stores of the new sausage entrepreneurs.

Those who remained continued to wait heroically. When the new stores opened, not with 333, but only 10 types of sausage, the line split up into 10 small lines. It turned out that people could *choose* their sausage. The Soviet line couldn't handle the ordeal of choice. When another novelty like "Snickers" or "Bounty" appeared on store shelves, queues rapidly shortened. The massive influx of German beer, Royal liquor, and women's stockings simply did it in, and the line caved.

The collapse of the line was much more painful for the collective Soviet body than the collapse of the Soviet Union. With the loss of the queue people lost an important therapeutic ritual of self-acknowledgment which had been honed and polished over the course of decades and had become a daily necessity, like drugs for an addict. Then, suddenly, there were no drugs. The collective body experienced a terrible withdrawal: furious demonstrations under red flags began, evolving into desperate clashes with the police, the ridiculous attempt at the first coup, newspapers shrieking about an "American occupation of Russia," the mass conversion of former communists to Russian Orthodoxy, and the creation of Committees for National Salvation from the Antichrist to Coca-Cola, etc. But all of this could not compensate for the loss of the line—the absinthian agony was too painful. The collective body grew smaller every day and, like some living Blob in a horror film, it frantically tried to figure out what else to transform itself into.

Its last incarnation was the Supreme Soviet of Russia. On September 21, 1993, Yeltsin dissolved the Collective Body. Hollywood-style convulsions began: red-brown goo oozed over the white marble of Moscow's White House, crowd scenes sprang up, the area of the film shoot was solidly cordoned off. Soon, as the genre requires to terrify the viewer, the blob broke through the cordon. It dribbled into trucks and set off to capture the television station, probably wanting to burble to the whole world: Give us back our Queue!

On October 4 the third and last signal event in the life of the Collective Body took place. Several tank salvos put an end to its history.

The wounded blob/monster was evacuated from the burned White House; the evacuation took the form of that very same queue. Not a small one either. Watching the holdout members of the Supreme Soviet file out of the White House, one's heart sank. The era of the "Great Standing Masses" was departing, departing forever. Every departure, especially under the barrel of a gun and with hands raised, provokes nostalgia. You start remembering things. But not the number on your hand, not the elbows in your ribs, not the hysterical cries: "Only three per person!" You remember other things. Pleasant things.

1971. The beginning of summer. Moscow is awash in poplar down. I'm fifteen years old. There's an extraordinary event near our apartment on Lenin Prospect: the neighborhood store, *Fish*, has black caviar. There's a small line, about a two-hour wait. I'm standing in it. My parents are away, on the Black Sea. I have a ton of money—forty rubles. For half this sum I can buy a kilo of caviar and treat my girlfriend Masha. About an hour and a half later I reach the counter, but some corpulent caviarophiles push me out of the line. One more minute and the death sentence will sound: "Boy," someone will say, "you weren't standing here." But I'm saved by our neighbor, nick-named Pear for the extraordinary shape of her body, which widens down below. With two swerves of her enormous ass she shoves the people at the head of the line and pushes me back to the counter.

"One kilo!" I exhale, thrusting forward my fist with the crumpled twenty rubles.

"Our norm is half a kilo!" the sweaty salesgirl brays at my face.

"Give him a fucking kilo, goddammit!" Pear shouts for the whole store to hear; turning to the line, she adds for appearance sake, a placating explanation: "They've got a regular infirmary at home! Everyone's sick!" The salesgirl belligerently tosses two greasy paper packages at my chest. Each contains half a kilo of black caviar. Hugging them, I make my way out of the store and on to the street, turn the corner, and go up to Masha's window. It's open. A breeze flutters the curtain.

"Masha," I call.

Masha appears. She's wearing a sleeveless dress of light, silvery silk. I show her my trophies. Smiling, she taps a finger to her temple.

Soon we are sitting on the windowsill. Between us in a porcelain soup bowl is a mountain of black caviar. We eat it by the spoonful, wash it down with warm lemon soda, and kiss with salty lips. . . .

Where is it all?

Where is the poplar down? Where is Masha? Where is the caviar?

Farewell to the Line.

Comrades, who's last in the queue?

—VLADIMIR SOROKIN
Translated from the Russian by Jamey Gambrell

TITLES IN SERIES

J.R. ACKERLEY Hindoo Holiday
J.R. ACKERLEY My Dog Tulip
J.R. ACKERLEY My Father and Myself
HENRY ADAMS The Jeffersonian Transformation
CÉLESTE ALBARET Monsieur Proust
DANTE ALIGHIERI The Inferno
DANTE ALIGHIERI The New Life
WILLIAM ATTAWAY Blood on the Forge
W.H. AUDEN (EDITOR) The Living Thoughts of Kierkegaard
W.H. AUDEN W. H. Auden's Book of Light Verse
ERICH AUERBACH Dante: Poet of the Secular World
DOROTHY BAKER Cassandra at the Wedding
J.A. BAKER The Peregrine
HONORÉ DE BALZAC The Unknown Masterpiece *and* Gambara
MAX BEERBOHM Seven Men
ALEXANDER BERKMAN Prison Memoirs of an Anarchist
GEORGES BERNANOS Mouchette
ADOLFO BIOY CASARES Asleep in the Sun
ADOLFO BIOY CASARES The Invention of Morel
CAROLINE BLACKWOOD Corrigan
CAROLINE BLACKWOOD Great Granny Webster
MALCOLM BRALY On the Yard
JOHN HORNE BURNS The Gallery
ROBERT BURTON The Anatomy of Melancholy
CAMARA LAYE The Radiance of the King
GIROLAMO CARDANO The Book of My Life
J.L. CARR A Month in the Country
BLAISE CENDRARS Moravagine
EILEEN CHANG Love in a Fallen City
UPAMANYU CHATTERJEE English, August: An Indian Story
NIRAD C. CHAUDHURI The Autobiography of an Unknown Indian
ANTON CHEKHOV Peasants and Other Stories
RICHARD COBB Paris and Elsewhere
COLETTE The Pure and the Impure
JOHN COLLIER Fancies and Goodnights
IVY COMPTON-BURNETT A House and Its Head
IVY COMPTON-BURNETT Manservant and Maidservant
BARBARA COMYNS The Vet's Daughter
EVAN S. CONNELL The Diary of a Rapist
HAROLD CRUSE The Crisis of the Negro Intellectual
ASTOLPHE DE CUSTINE Letters from Russia
LORENZO DA PONTE Memoirs
ELIZABETH DAVID A Book of Mediterranean Food
ELIZABETH DAVID Summer Cooking
MARIA DERMOÛT The Ten Thousand Things
DER NISTER The Family Mashber
ARTHUR CONAN DOYLE The Exploits and Adventures of Brigadier Gerard
CHARLES DUFF A Handbook on Hanging
ELAINE DUNDY The Dud Avocado
G.B. EDWARDS The Book of Ebenezer Le Page
EURIPIDES Grief Lessons: Four Plays; translated by Anne Carson
J.G. FARRELL Troubles

*For a complete list of titles, visit www.nyrb.com or write to:
Catalog Requests, NYRB, 435 Hudson Street, New York, NY 10014*

J.G. FARRELL The Siege of Krishnapur

J.G. FARRELL The Singapore Grip

KENNETH FEARING The Big Clock

KENNETH FEARING Clark Gifford's Body

FÉLIX FÉNÉON Novels in Three Lines

M.I. FINLEY The World of Odysseus

EDWIN FRANK (EDITOR) Unknown Masterpieces

CARLO EMILIO GADDA That Awful Mess on the Via Merulana

MAVIS GALLANT Paris Stories

MAVIS GALLANT Varieties of Exile

THÉOPHILE GAUTIER My Fantoms

JEAN GENET Prisoner of Love

JOHN GLASSCO Memoirs of Montparnasse

P. V. GLOB The Bog People: Iron-Age Man Preserved

EDMOND AND JULES DE GONCOURT Pages from the Goncourt Journals

EDWARD GOREY (EDITOR) The Haunted Looking Glass

A.C. GRAHAM Poems of the Late T'ang

VASILY GROSSMAN Life and Fate

OAKLEY HALL Warlock

PATRICK HAMILTON The Slaves of Solitude

PATRICK HAMILTON Twenty Thousand Streets Under the Sky

PETER HANDKE A Sorrow Beyond Dreams

ELIZABETH HARDWICK Seduction and Betrayal

ELIZABETH HARDWICK Sleepless Nights

L.P. HARTLEY Eustace and Hilda: A Trilogy

L.P. HARTLEY The Go-Between

NATHANIEL HAWTHORNE Twenty Days with Julian & Little Bunny by Papa

JANET HOBHOUSE The Furies

HUGO VON HOFMANNSTHAL The Lord Chandos Letter

JAMES HOGG The Private Memoirs and Confessions of a Justified Sinner

RICHARD HOLMES Shelley: The Pursuit

ALISTAIR HORNE A Savage War of Peace: Algeria 1954–1962

WILLIAM DEAN HOWELLS Indian Summer

RICHARD HUGHES A High Wind in Jamaica

RICHARD HUGHES In Hazard

RICHARD HUGHES The Fox in the Attic (The Human Predicament, Vol. 1)

RICHARD HUGHES The Wooden Shepherdess (The Human Predicament, Vol. 2)

MAUDE HUTCHINS Victorine

HENRY JAMES The Ivory Tower

HENRY JAMES The New York Stories of Henry James

HENRY JAMES The Other House

HENRY JAMES The Outcry

TOVE JANSSON The Summer Book

RANDALL JARRELL (EDITOR) Randall Jarrell's Book of Stories

DAVID JONES In Parenthesis

ERNST JÜNGER The Glass Bees

HELEN KELLER The World I Live In

FRIGYES KARINTHY A Journey Round My Skull

YASHAR KEMAL Memed, My Hawk

YASHAR KEMAL They Burn the Thistles

MURRAY KEMPTON Part of Our Time: Some Ruins and Monuments of the Thirties

DAVID KIDD Peking Story

ROBERT KIRK The Secret Commonwealth of Elves, Fauns, and Fairies
ARUN KOLATKAR Jejuri
TÉTÉ-MICHEL KPOMASSIE An African in Greenland
GYULA KRÚDY Sunflower
PATRICK LEIGH FERMOR Between the Woods and the Water
PATRICK LEIGH FERMOR Mani: Travels in the Southern Peloponnese
PATRICK LEIGH FERMOR Roumeli: Travels in Northern Greece
PATRICK LEIGH FERMOR A Time of Gifts
PATRICK LEIGH FERMOR A Time to Keep Silence
D.B. WYNDHAM LEWIS AND CHARLES LEE (EDITORS) The Stuffed Owl:
An Anthology of Bad Verse
GEORG CHRISTOPH LICHTENBERG The Waste Books
H.P. LOVECRAFT AND OTHERS The Colour Out of Space
ROSE MACAULAY The Towers of Trebizond
NORMAN MAILER Miami and the Siege of Chicago
JANET MALCOLM In the Freud Archives
OSIP MANDELSTAM The Selected Poems of Osip Mandelstam
GUY DE MAUPASSANT Afloat
JAMES McCOURT Mawrdew Czgowchwz
HENRI MICHAUX Miserable Miracle
JESSICA MITFORD Hons and Rebels
NANCY MITFORD Madame de Pompadour
ALBERTO MORAVIA Boredom
ALBERTO MORAVIA Contempt
JAN MORRIS Conundrum
ÁLVARO MUTIS The Adventures and Misadventures of Maqroll
L.H. MYERS The Root and the Flower
DARCY O'BRIEN A Way of Life, Like Any Other
YURI OLESHA Envy
IONA AND PETER OPIE The Lore and Language of Schoolchildren
RUSSELL PAGE The Education of a Gardener
BORIS PASTERNAK, MARINA TSVETAYEVA, AND RAINER MARIA RILKE
Letters: Summer 1926
CESARE PAVESE The Moon and the Bonfires
CESARE PAVESE The Selected Works of Cesare Pavese
LUIGI PIRANDELLO The Late Mattia Pascal
ANDREY PLATONOV Soul and Other Stories
J.F. POWERS Morte d'Urban
J.F. POWERS The Stories of J. F. Powers
J.F. POWERS Wheat That Springeth Green
CHRISTOPHER PRIEST Inverted World
RAYMOND QUENEAU We Always Treat Women Too Well
RAYMOND QUENEAU Witch Grass
RAYMOND RADIGUET Count d'Orgel's Ball
JEAN RENOIR Renoir, My Father
GREGOR VON REZZORI Memoirs of an Anti-Semite
TIM ROBINSON Stones of Aran: Pilgrimage
FR. ROLFE Hadrian the Seventh
WILLIAM ROUGHEAD Classic Crimes
CONSTANCE ROURKE American Humor: A Study of the National Character
GERSHOM SCHOLEM Walter Benjamin: The Story of a Friendship
DANIEL PAUL SCHREBER Memoirs of My Nervous Illness

JAMES SCHUYLER Alfred and Guinevere
JAMES SCHUYLER What's for Dinner?
LEONARDO SCIASCIA The Day of the Owl
LEONARDO SCIASCIA Equal Danger
LEONARDO SCIASCIA The Moro Affair
LEONARDO SCIASCIA To Each His Own
LEONARDO SCIASCIA The Wine-Dark Sea
VICTOR SEGALEN René Leys
VICTOR SERGE The Case of Comrade Tulayev
VICTOR SERGE Unforgiving Years
SHCHEDRIN The Golovlyov Family
GEORGES SIMENON Dirty Snow
GEORGES SIMENON The Engagement
GEORGES SIMENON The Man Who Watched Trains Go By
GEORGES SIMENON Monsieur Monde Vanishes
GEORGES SIMENON Red Lights
GEORGES SIMENON The Strangers in the House
GEORGES SIMENON Three Bedrooms in Manhattan
GEORGES SIMENON Tropic Moon
GEORGES SIMENON The Widow
CHARLES SIMIC Dime-Store Alchemy: The Art of Joseph Cornell
MAY SINCLAIR Mary Olivier: A Life
TESS SLESINGER The Unpossessed: A Novel of the Thirties
VLADIMIR SOROKIN Ice
VLADIMIR SOROKIN The Queue
CHRISTINA STEAD Letty Fox: Her Luck
GEORGE R. STEWART Names on the Land: A Historical Account of Place-Naming in the United States
STENDHAL The Life of Henry Brulard
ADALBERT STIFTER Rock Crystal
HOWARD STURGIS Belchamber
ITALO SVEVO As a Man Grows Older
HARVEY SWADOS Nights in the Gardens of Brooklyn
A.J.A. SYMONS The Quest for Corvo
TATYANA TOLSTAYA The Slynx
TATYANA TOLSTAYA White Walls: Collected Stories
EDWARD JOHN TRELAWNY Records of Shelley, Byron, and the Author
LIONEL TRILLING The Liberal Imagination
LIONEL TRILLING The Middle of the Journey
IVAN TURGENEV Virgin Soil
JULES VALLÈS The Child
MARK VAN DOREN Shakespeare
CARL VAN VECHTEN The Tiger in the House
ELIZABETH VON ARNIM The Enchanted April
EDWARD LEWIS WALLANT The Tenants of Moonbloom
ROBERT WALSER Jakob von Gunten
ROBERT WALSER Selected Stories
REX WARNER Men and Gods
SYLVIA TOWNSEND WARNER Lolly Willowes
SYLVIA TOWNSEND WARNER Mr. Fortune's Maggot *and* The Salutation
ALEKSANDER WAT My Century
C.V. WEDGWOOD The Thirty Years War

SIMONE WEIL AND RACHEL BESPALOFF War and the Iliad
GLENWAY WESCOTT Apartment in Athens
GLENWAY WESCOTT The Pilgrim Hawk
REBECCA WEST The Fountain Overflows
EDITH WHARTON The New York Stories of Edith Wharton
PATRICK WHITE Riders in the Chariot
T.H. WHITE The Goshawk
JOHN WILLIAMS Butcher's Crossing
JOHN WILLIAMS Stoner
ANGUS WILSON Anglo-Saxon Attitudes
EDMUND WILSON Memoirs of Hecate County
EDMUND WILSON To the Finland Station
RUDOLF AND MARGARET WITKOWER Born Under Saturn
GEOFFREY WOLFF Black Sun
STEFAN ZWEIG Beware of Pity
STEFAN ZWEIG Chess Story
STEFAN ZWEIG The Post-Office Girl